FISH HEADS

Also by Leonard Schonberg

Deadly Indian Summer

FISH HEADS

Leonard Schonberg

SUNSTONE
PRESS

*The events, people, and incidents in this story are the
sole product of the author's imagination.
The story is fictional and any resemblance to individuals
living or dead is purely coincidental.*

Sunstone books may be purchased for educational, business, or sales promotional use. For information please write: Special Markets Department, Sunstone Press, P.O. Box 2321, Santa Fe, New Mexico 87504-2321.

FIRST EDITION

Library of Congress Cataloging-in-Publication Data:

Schonberg, Leonard, 1935–
        Fish heads / Leonard Schonberg.—1st ed.
                p. cm.
        ISBN 0-86534-290-3 (hardcover) ISBN 978-1-63293-143-6 (softcover)
        I. Title.
    PS3569/ C5258F57   1999
    813' .54—dc21   99-30022
                                        CIP

Published by SUNSTONE PRESS
              Post Office Box 2321
              Santa Fe, NM 87504-2321 / USA
              (505) 988-4418 / *orders only* (800) 243-5644
              FAX (505) 988-1025
              www.sunstonepress.com

For Anne, with love

<u>ONE</u>

Mero Attri grunted with satisfaction as the outboard engine caught on the first pull.

He eased the boat away from the crumbling dock and waved to his two sons, who watched from the shore. The boys, five and seven, often followed him, hoping their father would take them along when he went fishing. Mero hated to refuse them anything but he now motioned them to return home.

The morning's unpredictable weather would require all his attention. There were times when, against his better judgement, he succumbed to their beseeching looks and let them clamber into the boat, but this particular morning was not one of them.

It had rained heavily during the night and now, as the first light of dawn appeared, black clouds were visible in the distance. There would be more rain before he could get his fishing lines into the water. The trade winds were blowing at fifteen or twenty knots and he fixed his attention on the whitecaps beyond the reef. Rough water, he thought, too rough to take the boys out, but good for fishing.

He steered toward the opening in the reef, feeling the surge of the tide when he was still fifty yards away. Off to his right the surf pounded on the reef, hurling foam and spray into the air. He glanced back toward Illeto's north shore and spotted his sons walking slowly toward their thatched house, barely visible behind the coconut palms lining the beach.

Tima, his wife, would be getting up about now to nurse the baby. He thought of their lovemaking during the night and smiled. After eight years, she was as passionate as she had been during their first days together. Mero knew he had been fortunate in his choice of a woman.

As Mero left the protection of the lagoon, the bow of his boat lifted into the air and then thudded into the trough between the waves. The sea was running at three to four feet, nothing his boat couldn't handle. The wooden craft, a sixteen-footer, was twelve years old, but not for a moment did Mero doubt its seaworthiness. He had purchased it from an American on Kwajalein who was being transferred back to the United States. It had taken all the money he had saved during the two years he worked at the American missile-tracking base but it was worth it. His "boum-boum," as the islanders called it because of its noisy engine, made it possible for him to go farther and faster into the deeper ocean waters. In recent years, as the Marshallese government had leased its rich fishing grounds to Asians and Americans, Mero often found it necessary to head further offshore in search of tuna. The traditional flat-bottomed Marshallese canoes were better suited for the rocky, shallow waters of the lagoon and reef, waters that no longer provided the bounty of the past.

Propelled by the seventy-five horsepower motor he had bought with the money his sister, Jotai, had given him, Mero's boat sliced easily through the waves. There wasn't much to be thankful to the Americans for, but he knew that without them he would not have his boat or the outboard. Mero's family had owned land on Kwajalein; when his mother died, his sister, in accordance with Marshallese tradition, had inherited the land. The Marshallese living on Kwajalein had been relocated by the Americans to the nearby island of Ebeye after the Second World War. There they were condemned to live in poverty, thousands crowded onto less than a square mile of living space, totally dependent on the Americans for work and sustenance. Mero's sister was more fortunate than most. The Americans paid rent to her for her land on Kwajalein and she and her brother lived on the island of Illetto, far from the squalor of Ebeye. The Americans' rent money had made it possible for him to buy his motor.

Scanning the horizon, he saw dolphins arching out of the water about a mile away. That was the area he would fish. The dark clouds were now directly above him and released a sudden downpour. Mero, his attention focused on the dolphins, ignored the warm rainwater streaming down his face and bare chest. Ten minutes later, the rain was gone and the sun appeared above the eastern horizon. Cumulus clouds scudded before the wind and, for the moment at least, there were no rain clouds visible. At this time of year the showers could appear at any time but were usually of short duration.

As Mero drew closer to the spot where he had first seen the dolphins, he was surprised to see the usually sociable creatures moving away. Ordinarily they would encircle his boat, some stationing themselves as leaders at the bow while the rest capered on all sides, leaping and plunging back into the water. He peered closely at the ocean surface looking for shark fins, but none were visible. This group may have calves, he thought. Dolphin young suckle almost hourly for the first few weeks and continue to nurse for at least a year. Since there was no apparent threat from sharks, it was the only explanation he could come up with for their strange behavior.

Mero tried to approach but the dolphins maintained their distance. He scanned the horizon, looking for anything he might have missed. His initial puzzlement was now replaced with a feeling of unease; it was as if the dolphins were trying to warn him not to come near. They must have calves, he thought, trying to reassure himself. Above him, the sky suddenly darkened again. The wind, which had increased, carried the smell of rain. He wondered why he had not noticed the sudden change. A few terns which had followed in his wake almost from the time he left shore now wheeled about and flew back in the direction from which they had come. Mero prided himself on his ability to read the vagaries of the ocean and the moods of the tropical winds. Now he felt strangely discomfited. Even as he opened the engine's throttle, trying to narrow the distance between the dolphins and himself, he wondered if he should change course, perhaps even return to shore.

But these thoughts ended abruptly as the boat was suddenly jarred by a sharp impact. Immediately, the engine stopped and the craft rocked in the waves. Mero, gathering his wits, jumped from his seat and moved quickly to the bow. He slowly leaned over the edge, the boat rising and falling beneath him. His first thought was that he had collided with a dolphin, an overly curious straggler left behind. Seeing nothing, he moved to the starboard side. Here tendrils of blood snaked past, just beneath the ocean's surface. Mero stooped to maintain his balance and sidled cautiously toward the outboard motor. Carefully placing his hands on the edge of the boat, he leaned over the stern. Blood streamed from the propeller. Something was caught in the blades.

He reached down and, in horror, pulled up a human arm. At the severed end were torn muscles and blood vessels and bone; all had been cut through by the propeller blades. Dear God, thought Mero, I've hit a swimmer. Stunned, he dropped the arm on the deck and lurched from one side of the boat to the other, searching the water for the victim.

A grey-black object floated by and Mero lunged for it, almost tipping the boat. This time he pulled up what appeared to be a dolphin head, jagged and bleeding where it, also, had encountered the propeller's blades. Mero had never seen a blowhole so close to a dolphin's snout, but that was not what seized his attention. The eyes, open and staring as if surprised by what had happened, were like no eyes he had ever seen on a fish or sea mammal: they were human. Mero gasped and violently threw the head to the deck. He slumped down on the cross seat, his bowels cramped in fright, staring wildly at the bloody parts. For the first time he noticed the hand, its fingers long and webbed with no nails visible.

Mero instantly crossed himself and then vomited over the side. When he had gained control, he forced himself to continue searching the water. But if there were any other parts, the waves had carried them away. No sharks had yet been attracted by the blood, but he knew they would not be long in coming. In the distance he could still see the dolphins, but they were no longer moving away from him.

Mero frantically pulled at the engine cord but the motor would not start. Twice he forced himself to reach into the dark water and feel around the blades to make certain that they were not jammed. Then, on the fourth try, the motor roared to life. Mero instantly swung the boat around toward the shore. The rain had stopped and the sun was well above the horizon but there would be no fishing today. He could think only of the creature he had killed.

He deliberately kept his eyes away from the remains on the deck, fixing his gaze on the approaching shoreline as he frantically forced the boat at high speed through the waves. Casting a quick glance over his shoulder, he could make out the dolphins moving toward the spot of his bloody collision. It was as if they were coming back for something. But what could this creature, this monstrosity, have to do with them?

Mero, a devout Catholic, crossed himself again. And then he remembered an incident of two months ago. It was just before the birth of his new daughter. His wife, Tima, had accompanied his sons to the boat on a morning when he promised to take the boys fishing. "Come with us," Mero said to his wife. Tima hesitated. Marshallese women only fished from shore. It was considered bad luck to go on board a fishing boat. "Come on," he said. "You don't believe those silly superstitions." A few neighbors who were on the beach ran toward them. "What are you doing?" they cried to Tima. "You mustn't go out fishing with your man." Mero had laughed at them. Taking his wife's hand he urged her into the boat. They left their neighbors pleading for them to come back. Tima, using one of Mero's best fishing poles, had even caught a tuna that day.

Now Mero remembered that day with shame. Catholic though he was, he should never have gone against the beliefs of his people.

Black rainclouds filled the sky as Mero approached the reef. Steering into the inlet, he wondered what he would tell his wife and neighbors. Tima, he knew, would be terrified. She would believe a curse had been put on them. And the neighbors, certain that the evil eye was upon Mero and Tima because of their transgression, would ostracize them. It was best, he decided, to say nothing. He cut his speed as he entered the lagoon. Keeping away from the shore, he continued eastward past his customary docking point, toward the other end of the island. There he hoped to find the one person who might be able to help him.

TWO

The clinic on Illetto was a one-room shack with plywood walls and tin-sheet roofing, the only structure of its kind on the island. The one-hundred nine Marshallese who called the island home still lived in houses constructed entirely of thatch. Two wooden tables, stretching for six feet when placed end to end and covered with a woven mat, served as an examining table for Jodi Larsen, the U.S. Public Health Service physician serving a one-month assignment on the island.

Shining her flashlight on the feet of the woman lying on the table, she examined them carefully. "You have an ulcer forming on the sole of your right foot," she said. "That can be very dangerous for you. If you don't keep your diabetes under control and help this ulcer to heal, it can lead to gangrene."

After serving a year at the hospital in Ebeye, Jodi Larsen's Marshallese, a language the islanders called Kajin Majel, was fluent. Still, she had to search for words when trying to explain illness to her patients. The diseases now afflicting the Marshallese had not existed prior to the establishment of American military bases on the islands. This was primarily due to the change in their diet. Instead of their traditional foods—fish, breadfruit, coconut and bananas—the majority now subsisted on rice and sugar-laden junkfood. As a result, obesity, diabetes and high blood pressure were major health problems. The Marshallese, with a third of the population affected, now had the highest incidence of diabetes in the world.

Jodi's patient, a markedly overweight woman of thirty-five, nodded and smiled when Jodi talked to her about diet. But Jodi knew what was on the shelves of the island's small store and that Coca Cola and Sugar Pops would always win out over coconut milk and bananas.

She told the woman to stay off her feet as much as possible and to use warm soaks so that the ulcer could heal. At this, the woman laughed uproariously and pointed to the doorway of the clinic. A crowd of small children stood there, jostling one another to peer into the room.

"All yours?" Jodi asked.

"Yes," she said, still laughing.

"I guess rest is a word you don't know," said Jodi, laughing with her. "Are you taking the pills for your diabetes?"

"Sometimes I forget."

"It's very important," said Jodi. "If gangrene develops, you could lose your foot. In the hospital in Ebeye, there are many women whose feet have been amputated. If that happens, how will you take care of your children?"

The woman, like many of the diabetic patients she encountered, should be on insulin, Jodi knew, but with no refrigeration on most of the islands, that wasn't possible.

"I will take the pills," promised the woman, sliding off the table.

"Kommool tata," she called to Jodi as she shooed her children out of the doorway.

"Thank you very much."

Jodi shook her head sadly. At times, she wondered if her presence on the island made the slightest difference. The Public Health Service appeared to think that by sending one of their physicians from Ebeye or Mejato to Illetto twice a year, for a month each time, they were providing the islanders with adequate medical care. But the problems were too great and the means of treatment too meagre.

She walked over to the bookcase where her medicines were stored. They filled only half of one shelf. Pills for diabetes, some tubes of antibiotic ointment, over-the-counter painkillers, a bottle of antibiotic tablets, Betadine, rubbing alcohol and several ampules of Depo-Provera for the few women on the island who requested a birth control method. That was the extent of her pharmacy.

Jodi was particularly disturbed by the number of thyroid nodules she had found in the first two weeks she had been on Illetto. When H-Bomb Bravo was detonated on Bikini atoll in 1954, fallout from the bomb was carried eastward by the winds to Rongelap and Utrik. The people on those islands had been evacuated and followed medically on a regular basis by physicians sent out every year by Haverbrook, a research facility in Boston under contract to the U.S. Department of Energy. That followup had revealed an alarming number of cases of thyroid abnormalities, including nodules that sometimes progressed to cancer.

Illetto, even closer to Bikini than Rongelap, had been considered an uninhabited island in 1954. What Jodi had discovered inadvertantly was that a number of Marshallese had been on Illetto during the H-Bomb test. Lekoj Kel, the present owner of the Illetto store, was one of them.

Only two days earlier, Kel, a man now in his sixties, had been sitting in front of his store talking with Jodi about the changes he had seen in his forty-five years on the island.

"But no one lived here then," said Jodi. "Didn't people only begin living here about thirty-five years ago?"

"There were always people here," Kel replied quietly. "They just didn't live here all the time back then. I used to come here with others from Ailinginae atoll when I was a boy to gather the eggs of sea birds and the coconuts, which were better than those on our islands. There were almost fifty of us here the day the sun rose in both the east and the west."

Jodi had heard that same description from some of the Rongelap people on Ebeye.

They had awakened on March 1, 1954 to see what appeared to be sunrise in the west, the area of the H-Bomb detonation, and shortly afterwards a second sunrise, the expected one, in the east. They still referred to it as the day of two suns.

Puzzled, Jodi stared fixedly at the bronze-skinned man. "Were the Americans aware that you were here?"

"No," he replied. "We never told them. We were frightened and sailed back to our island that same day. It was many years until my people returned and began to live here. As you say, that was about thirty-five years ago."

"But, Mister Kel, you and the others may have been exposed to high levels of radiation. Shouldn't you have told the Americans?"

The storeowner lowered his head. "It was foolish of me to have told you this. Doctor, please, you must say nothing to anyone. You know that the people of Rongelap and Utrik were removed from their islands. The Rongelapese are still not back on their own island and more than forty years have passed since Bravo. You have seen how the people live on Ebeye and I can tell you how they live on Mejato. On Mejato, the fishing is very bad and there are few trees. On Ebeye, thirteen thousand people live in squalor on land that was meant for hundreds. We are happy here on Illetto. There are not many of us and we have decent fishing and trees that give us coconuts and breadfruit. We don't want to move."

"I understand how you feel about the island," said Jodi. "It is beautiful. But what if the soil is still contaminated? What if the fish are contaminated? Mister Kel, I'm only on Illetto for a month. I'm not concerned with any short-term exposure to radiation that I may be getting. But you and the other islanders have been here for years. It's best to make certain that there are no high levels of radiation."

"Doctor Jodi, you ask what if? To find the answers to what if, we would be moved from this island. That is what we do not want. And there is something else you must think about. You have been in the Marshall Islands long enough, I think, to know something about politics here. Our government is almost bankrupt. It depends on the United States for everything. If Americans like you did not come to this island, the people here would never see a doctor. Your country now says it is safe for the people of Rongelap to live on their island, but our government says that is not true. People in the government are saying that other islands were contaminated, islands never mentioned by the Americans. They say the United States should give more money so that these islands and the people living on them can be studied.

"If my government found out some of the people living here had been on the island during the Bravo blast, they would make a big political issue of it. We would have to move. Any money received by the Marshallese government from your country would never be seen by the people exposed to fallout. That is the sad truth. So we prefer to take our chances and remain here.

"You have been on Illetto for only a few weeks and you have seen some of the health problems. We cannot blame everything on fallout. I know you are thinking that I am partially responsible because of the foods I sell to the people. But you must remember that I sell them what they want. Some of these people have worked at the American bases on Kwajalein and Roi-Namur. Others have relatives working there.

They have grown accustomed to the foods of the Americans. On Illetto we are more fortunate than the people on other islands. We still have good foods here. We have fish and we have fruit. Our people are much better off than those on Ebeye and Mejato."

"I'll think about what you've said, Mister Kel. I must go now and see some patients."

For the rest of that day, Jodi was distracted by those revelations. She didn't realize until that same evening how troubled Lekoj Kel was by what he had divulged. As palm fronds rustled in the night breezes that came off the ocean, Jodi sat at a makeshift desk in one corner of her hut. The thatched structure belonged to an elderly couple who were visiting family in Ebeye. It had been given to Jodi to use.

A kerosene lantern sat on the small table. She was now deeply immersed in the chapter on thyroid diseases in her endocrinology textbook. It was almost eight o'clock when she heard Kel's voice outside.

"May we speak to you, Doctor Jodi?" he asked.

"Of course," she said, going to the door. Raising her lantern above her head, she made out the familiar face of the storeowner. "Who is that with you?"

"It is Mister Monna."

Jodi had not seen him since the day she arrived. He was the unofficial headman of the island and had greeted her when she stepped off the boat that had brought her from Bikini. Mister Monna followed Kel into the hut and stepped up to Jodi. He clasped her hand in greeting in both of his own. His hands were gnarled from age and work, but strong. He was the oldest person on the island although, like most Marshallese, he was unaware of his exact age. Jodi guessed he was close to eighty.

"It's nice to see you again. Please sit down—both of you." She motioned to the woven mats on the smooth sand floor and sat down facing them.

Monna cleared his throat and spoke softly. Jodi had to listen closely to hear his words.

"My friend, Kel, informs me that he has told you some things he perhaps should not have. He did not mean to put you in a difficult position."

16

"I'm glad Mister Kel did tell me, Mister Monna. It helps to explain the thyroid nodules I've been finding in some of the people. If they were on Illetto during the blast, it would indicate they had heavy exposure to fallout. I realize, Mister Monna, that Illetto is somewhat south of the fallout path from Bravo, but not by much. There may have been as much, or more, fallout here than on Rongelap. Were you with Mister Kel on Illetto during Bravo?"

"Yes. I was here harvesting coconuts. Kel and I came together in my canoe."

"The people who were on Rongelap say the fallout came as yellow powder. Some children thought it was snow and played in it. Did you see anything like that here?"

The headman cast a quick glance at Kel and shook his head unconvincingly. "No. We were frightened by the sunrise in the west and left the island shortly after that."

A light rain was now falling and they sat listening to the play of the drops on the roof of the hut. Monna broke the silence. "I would like you to forget what we have discussed. It would be best for my people."

Jodi looked into the old man's lined face. His rheumy eyes met hers. "If only I could be sure of that, Mister Monna. I can't promise anything, but for the time being I'll say nothing."

Monna nodded and slowly got to his feet. Jodi, her lantern held high, followed the two men to the door. She watched their dark forms descend the path, then disappear among the palms. The rain stopped as abruptly as it had begun and a half-moon struggled to make its way from behind the clouds.

Jodi eased down on her cot and stared at the flickering light from the lamp. What a troubling day, she thought. First she had inadvert-ently discovered that people had been on the island during the Bravo H-Bomb test. And now two of the elders were asking for her silence.

Her immediate inclination was to refuse their request, and yet, having worked in the hospital on Ebeye for a year, Jodi could understand. Illetto was a beautiful island covered with palms and surrounded by the turquoise waters of a lagoon that still provided fish. The huts of the small population were scattered, ensuring privacy for the families. Ebeye, on the other hand, had hovels of plywood and metal jammed against one another, each filled with malnourished people. The waters around that island were contaminated by sewage and floating debris. Bottles, plastic sacks, vegetable rinds and dead rodents bobbed on the surface between tides.

Work for the rapidly expanding population was virtually non-existent, yet prices in the stores were higher than on Kwajalein. Diarrheal diseases were rampant, most due to inadequate sanitation. The hospital was underfunded by the Marshallese government and deteriorating rapidly. Money earmarked for the hospital, as well as supplies and pharmaceuticals, simply disappeared. Holes gaped in the stucco walls , the roof leaked, rats ran in the corridors and patients had to provide their own food and bedding.

In this setting, Jodi and the other foreign physicians working there had struggled to treat dysentery and typhoid, syphilis and meningitis, leprosy and diabetes. It was as bad, if not worse, than anything she had seen during her two-year Peace Corps stint in Malawi. The difference was that Malawi was in Africa. The Marshall Islands had been a United States trust territory from 1947 until independence in 1986, and even now was involved in a Compact of Free Association with America.

If she kept silent about Kel's revelation, the people of Illetto would continue living their tranquil existence. But what if the snake of nuclear radiation was loose in this Garden of Eden? What if the soil and the sea were contaminated? What if some of these islanders were already harboring the seeds of thyroid cancer and leukemia?

This night Jodi felt older than her thirty-three years. And she was a long way from her parents' farm in New Hampshire where she had grown up. As an only child in a remote area near the Canadian border she had depended on farm animals and pets for companionship. She idolized Doctor Rutherford, the elderly veterinarian who had cured her horse of colic and amputated her dog's leg after it had been crushed by her father's tractor.

Her dream, to follow in his footsteps, changed suddenly when she was fourteen. She had borrowed a copy of "Microbe Hunters" from her school library. Reading about Pasteur, Koch and Ehrlich provided her with a new pantheon of heroes. To Jodi's parents, her fantasy about becoming a physician rather than a vet was no more than that—a fantasy which they expected her to surrender as she got older. The life the Larsens envisioned for her didn't encompass more than being a wife and mother, and if she was insistent about getting educated beyond high school, they had repeatedly told her, it might as well be for something within reach, something practical like a schoolteacher, not a vet, and certainly not a doctor.

But if any word could describe Jodi Larsen it was tenacious. Medicine was her dream and it was one she refused to surrender. She easily won a scholarship to the University of New Hampshire and then to medical school in Massachusetts. After completing a residency in family practice, she earned a master's degree in public health at Columbia University.

For Jodi, being a physician meant service, not personal gain. Offers to join private practices flooded her mailbox, but she had loftier goals. To the dismay of her parents, who thought she would at least settle down close to them, she joined the Peace Corps and was sent to Malawi in southeast Africa. After two years there, she joined the U.S. Public Health Service.

While in Malawi, she had worked in villages near the border with Mozambique. More than once she had been caught up in the fighting between the Mozambique government and rebels as it spilled across the border. Villages she worked in had been bombarded and burned while Jodi, at no little risk to her own safety, continued giving intravenous drips and providing lifesaving solutions to children dying of malnutrition and diarrhea.

The Marshall Islands were tame in comparison. At least they had been until she discovered Illetto's secret.

How could she not divulge what she had learned? Was she willing to take responsibility for the leukemias and thryoid cancers that might develop as a result of the exposure to radioactive fallout? She wished there were someone she could talk to. But even when the time came for her to return to Kwajalein and Ebeye in a few weeks, she knew there would be no friend there to confide in.

Jodi often wondered about her lack of close friendships. At times she ascribed it to her lonely upbringing as a child; at other times she wondered if it was some defect in her own character. The closest she had come to finding a companion was while she was in her residency program at Mary Hitchcock Hospital. He was her senior resident and they had an easy openness almost from the beginning. Besides sharing a love for their work, they had the same passion for hiking and skiing.

It was only when they became seriously involved and began talking about a future together that Jodi realized they were on divergent paths. When his residency ended, he joined a group in Hanover, promising her there would be a position waiting when she finished and asking her to set a date for their marriage.

"Then, once we start having kids," he said, "I'll be well enough established so we'll only need the one income."

At that point, in a confrontation that ran from tears to shouting, Jodi abruptly cut it off. "It's just not what I envision for myself. I'm sorry," were her final words as she walked out the door.

She had dated an older man during her master's program at Columbia. He held a professorship at the college and was content with his work and with living in the city. But Jodi wanted more than that. She had already submitted her application to the Peace Corps. They drifted apart. The dissolution was amicable but no less painful.

Disappointed after these experiences, Jodi had shied away from further involvements. At the age of thirty-three she had reached the point where she no longer thought of marriage. An intimate relationship now meant a friend in whom she could confide, male or female. And that was something she did not have.

Jodi went to bed that evening trying to balance her concern for the people of Illetto with the pleas for silence from Kel and Monna. But by morning she was no closer to a solution. Frustrated, she got into her swimsuit and snatched her towel from the chair. Jodi usually swam for a half-hour before having breakfast. On this day she extended her swim, hoping that physical exertion would clear her mind.

Later that morning, while working in the clinic, Jodi made up her mind to concentrate solely on work for the weeks that remained on Illetto. There would be time when she returned to Kwajalein to decide whether or not to keep Kel's secret.

Since medical problems on Illetto were no worse than on the other islands, perhaps her concerns were exaggerated.

She had almost succeeded in convincing herself when John Muje, the fourteen-year-old son of one of her patients, came looking for her. She was in the clinic, treating a festering wound on the leg of one of his friends. The boy winced as Jodi drained the abscess. As she applied a clean gauze dressing, she noticed John standing in the doorway.

"Did you fall on coral, too?"

The boy shook his head. "Someone is looking for you."

"Who?"

"Mero Attri."

Jodi tried to place the name. "Oh, Mero the fisherman. Well, where is he? Is he hurt?"

"No," said John, coming closer to watch Jodi bandage his friend's leg. "I saw him on the beach and he sent me to get you."

"Why doesn't he come up here?"

The boy shrugged.

"Well, go tell Mero I'll be down in a few minutes. Where can I find him?"

The boy pointed directly behind the hut, then ran out the door.

Jodi turned to her young patient and helped him from the table. "Now don't get that wet. I want you to come back in three days so I can make sure it's healing."

Perplexed by the fisherman's request and exasperated at being summoned from the clinic for what did not appear to be an emergency, Jodi hastened down the path to the beach.

She had first met Mero only a few days after her arrival when he had come to her with a fish hook deeply embedded in his thumb. Fortunately, she had some Xylocaine, making it possible to remove it. She had wondered at the time what he would have done had there been no doctor on the island. When she asked him, the fisherman had laughed and made a sawing motion with his other hand. After that, she occasionally noticed him on his boat when she went for her early morning swim. Mero always waved.

She spotted the boat pulled up on the sand, the outboard lifted from the water. Mero was seated on the bow, his back to her.

"Another fish hook?" she asked.

Slowly he turned his head and looked at her with vacant eyes. Mero's mouth moved soundlessly and he was on the verge of tears.

"What is it?" she asked, alarmed. "Is someone in the family ill?"

He stood up shakily and stepped slowly out of the boat. Bending over, he grabbed at a sheet of canvas on the deck and threw it aside.

"I hit something when I was fishing." He quickly looked around to make certain no one was watching, then pointed into the boat.

Jodi stepped closer, then shrank back as he lifted a severed arm and motioned to the head.

"My God, what are these?"

Mero shook his head. "I don't know. I think I am being punished for bringing my wife out on the boat to fish. I was warned not to do that and didn't listen. Perhaps someone has cast a spell, someone who is jealous of my boat."

Jodi knew better than to take the fisherman's superstitions lightly. The Marshallese still retained their belief in the world of spirits. Most of her female patients even refused to have sex with their husbands during the full moon, believing it would bring bad luck and result in no fish being caught. More than once, her patients had hinted of spells being cast against them. Only a week before, a woman had tearfully complained to her that a neighbor was responsible for breaking up her family. She had seen her neighbor throw a shell in the ocean and another on the shore, and less than a month later, the woman's husband had left her.

Recovering from her initial shock, Jodi extended both hands to take the arm from the fisherman. She shuddered as she touched the cold skin. It was, except for the hand, a human arm, dangling shreds of torn muscle and fibrous tissue at its severed end. Sharp jagged edges protruded from the humerus, the shattered bone of the upper arm. But the hand? Long fingers without nails at the end and webbing between the fingers that stretched wide to permit greater than normal lateral movement.

Turning the arm over, trying to make sense of it, Jodi remembered reading in college that the earliest mammals had lived on land, not in the sea. Sixty million years ago some species of four-footed mammals had returned to the sea, the medium in which all primitive living creatures had their beginnings.

In a comparative anatomy textbook, she had seen X-rays of the flippers of cetaceans, the family to which dolphins belonged, those films revealing the bones of five "fingers," as well as what could be construed as wrist and arm bones. Like whales, dolphins were true warm-blooded mammalian creatures and the X-rays provided additional evidence of their land origins.

But this was a human arm, one that appeared to be undergoing a metamorphosis to make it more adaptable to sea life. If someone had told her that such a creature existed, she would have scoffed at it as fantasy.

The severed head was more typical of what she would have expected of a sea mammal, but there were inconsistencies. Lips and tongue were absent, but the blow hole was not high on the head. Instead, it was closer to the mouth, almost where one would expect nostrils. The eyes were the most disconcerting. She was struck, as Mero had been, by their resemblance to human eyes. No sea creature had eyes like these.

"Mero, where did you hit this . . . thing?"

"About a mile and a half offshore. I saw dolphins leaping from the water and thought I might find tuna there. Usually, dolphins will come right up to the boat, but these moved away. After I hit . . . it, I picked these parts up, then I headed back to Illetto. But I saw the dolphins returning to the spot where the boat had been. I've never seen dolphins behave like that."

"Have you told anyone about this? Or shown this to anyone?"

"No. I came to find you. You are an educated doctor and I thought you would know what it is."

"I don't, Mero. I wish I did, but I don't."

She could see the disappointment on his face.

"If the other people see this, they will ask Tima and me to leave the island. They will think we are cursed and will bring misfortune to them."

Hearing the desperation in his voice, Jodi put her hand on his shoulder. "Mero, you did well to bring these to me. It's a very important find and I'm only sorry it had to happen in such a terrible way. Even though I have no explanation, I think it would be best if you told no one about this. As you say, it would frighten the people. If it's all right with you, I would like to keep these parts and take them back to Kwajalein. Perhaps the scientists there will have some answers."

"Please," he said, now relieved. "You take them."

She helped him push the boat back into the water, where Mero started the engine and moved slowly away from the shore. He did not turn around for his customary wave.

Jodi walked quickly back to the clinic, gripping the severed arm in one hand and cradling the head grotesquely in her other arm. If only

I don't meet anyone, she thought. She paused behind the building and looked around. No one in sight. Although she would have preferred taking the parts to her hut, there was too much risk of meeting someone at this time of day.

She nudged the clinic door open with her shoulder, stooping to enter, and paused as she quietly closed the door behind her with her foot. Quickly, she crossed the room to a small cabinet where she kept syringes and materials for dressings. She placed the arm and head on the exam table as she emptied the shelves. Gingerly, she lifted the clammy parts and stored them on the shelves, knowing they could not remain there long. In the humid heat, the smell would quickly give them away.

Jodi slumped on the low stool before the small table she used as a desk. She glanced at the cabinet, half-expecting Mero's strange find to come tumbling out. The silence made her uncomfortable. Hoping no other patients would come looking for her that morning, Jodi left the clinic and headed to her hut. The two grisly objects were secure since no one would enter the building in her absence. The most important thing now was to have some time to think.

Jodi lowered herself onto her cot and closed her eyes. She could not dispel the images of that arm and the dolphin head, if that was what it was. She wondered if it was some isolated example of a strange mutation. Although mutations were not uncommon in nature, they could not be dismissed in an offhand way if they occurred in the Marshall Islands. After H-Bomb Bravo, there was a rash of abnormal pregnancies, most of them believed to be due to radiation from the fallout. Some women miscarried or had stillbirths. Others had babies with ghastly abnormalities and the Marshallese referred to them as "jellyfish babies." These malformed fetuses had been buried immediately after birth and the United States government still denied their existence.

But it was now more than forty years since Bravo. Was there still enough radiation in the waters around Illetto to cause such a mutation? There was no way for her to judge the age of the creature Mero had struck. If this wasn't an isolated example, how many other mutant creatures might be in the sea?

Jodi sat up abruptly, her head aching. There were too many questions. She slowly turned toward a radio resting on a wooden crate in one corner of her hut. This battery-operated unit, enabling her to contact the small American station on Bikini atoll or even Kwajalein depending on atmospheric conditions, had been given to her for emergencies. Perhaps it was stretching a bit to call this an emergency but she felt there was a sense of urgency. She could not simply let the parts sit. It was absolutely essential to get them to Kwajalein as quickly as possible. Once she placed her call, the personnel on Bikini would pick her up by boat, then fly her from their airstrip to Roi-Namur. From there she could catch one of the frequent flights to Kwajalein.

She wondered what reaction Mero's find would elicit from the Haverbrook staff. Tomorrow she would know.

THREE

The two women were complete contrasts. Jodi Larsen's ash-blond hair skimmed her shoulders. She had green eyes, a delicately freckled complexion and was often referred to as "that quiet blond woman" by those who didn't know her. Nothing striking, nothing out of the ordinary. But her passion for matters that interested her quickly dispelled any initial impression of a demure, retiring woman. She exuded an enthusiasm that was infectious and a listener, captivated by her ardent expression, would suddenly realize that she was beautiful.

There was nothing shy about Virginia Chambers. The woman standing opposite Jodi had a presence that filled the room. At least twenty years older than her and half a head taller, she was described by her colleagues as "one tough lady." The description was apt. Like Jodi, Doctor Chambers was a New Englander, born and raised in Brockton, Massachusetts. She was the only girl in a family of five brothers and learned at an early age that she could expect no favors based on gender. After completing her residency in internal medicine, she had enlisted in the army, something she would never have considered had she not been saddled with student loan debt.

In one of life's ironies, she had immediately been sent to Viet Nam, where the person who had been closest to her had been killed only four years earlier. There she served in a field hospital, maintaining her stone-faced composure as she treated the sick and wounded. After four years in the military, she joined the reserve and applied for a fellowship at Brigham in endocrinology. Recalled by the army during Desert Storm, she now held a commission as full colonel. She had followed the tanks into Iraq and garnered the respect of the men in her unit. Her fellow officers tiptoed warily around this imposing woman.

She wore her grey hair cut short with bangs in front. Her shoulders were rounded, as if trying to compensate for her height. This had the unintended effect of thrusting her head forward, giving her a predatory appearance that the rigid smile on her face did nothing to dispel.

When Doctor Chambers had left the army this second time, she was recruited by Haverbrook Laboratory in Boston and put in command of their Marshall Islands team. Twice a year, for a month at a time, she was at her post in Kwajalein, examining patients and compiling statistics on those who had been exposed to fallout from the American H-Bomb testing.

She and Jodi Larsen now stared at the arm and dolphin-like head lying on the table between them. Jodi had arrived on the early afternoon flight from Roi-Namur and gone immediately to the small base hospital, where she and Doctor Chambers were now closeted in a small, air-conditioned office with the door locked.

"Except for the fisherman," said Jodi, "no one on Illetto knows anything about this. I also got some disturbing news from a few of the elders. During Bravo, Illetto was considered uninhabited. But in reality there were at least fifty people from Ailinginae on the island. They were gathering coconuts and seabird eggs. The elders claim they left the island immediately after seeing the light of the blast and didn't see any fallout. But I'm not convinced. Those people may have received high doses of radiation. They're so afraid of being removed from Illetto that they begged me not to tell anyone about their being there."

Virginia Chambers pulled up a chair and sat down. She indicated for Jodi to do the same. Jodi had met the older woman briefly only once before, just prior to leaving for Illetto. There was something disconcerting about that rigid smile and the discomfort Jodi had felt at their initial meeting was now intensified.

"We know all about Illetto," Chambers said, the smile still frozen on her face.

"What do you mean?" Jodi asked, surprised.

"We knew there were people on the island during Bravo. Oh, I don't mean we knew immediately. But Haverbrook found it out about ten years later when the first thyroid abnormalities began to appear in the people who had been on Rongelap. About the same time physicians noticed thyroid nodules and cancers in people from

Ailinginae. At first, they weren't sure if that was related to Bravo because Ailinginae was somewhat south of the fallout path. And then, in talking to the people, they learned that some had been on Illetto when the bomb was detonated."

"The people now living on Illetto think the Americans don't know about it."

"That's because we want them to think that."

Jodi now found the ever-present smile hideous. "I don't understand."

"Doctor Larsen, there's more to consider here than medical findings. There's politics. I don't know how much of that you're aware of. You've spent a year on Ebeye so you must have some knowledge of the situation.

"Politics!" snapped Jodi. "Yes, I know about politics. Even the elders on Illetto talk about politics. But what has that got to do with people who were exposed to radiation? How do we know that radiation wasn't responsible for. . . that thing?" She pointed at the objects on the table between them.

"Look," said Chambers, cutting her off. "A mistake was made. It was during the fifties, remember, and we were in a nuclear race with the Russians. There were miscalculations as to blast intensity and wind direction. Bravo was to have been a five megaton blast. Instead, it was seventeen. That's more than a thousand times the force of the Hiroshima explosion. And yes, the wind that morning was blowing toward inhabited islands. Even some of our own personnel on Rongerik atoll were exposed."

"I know all that," said Jodi.

Virginia Chambers raised her hand. "Hear me out. Once we knew the people of Rongelap and Utrik had been exposed, they were evacuated. There was even a snafu there. Forty-eight hours had elapsed before the evacuations began. It wasn't only the Marshallese and some of our people who were exposed. There were also twenty-three Japanese fisherman on a tuna boat. They were a hundred miles east of Bikini when they were caught in the fallout. It took them two weeks to get back to Japan, during which they all developed radiation sickness. They arrived in Japan with their skin blistered and their hair falling out. One of them died. If there was one country that had a right to be sensitive about nuclear radiation, it was Japan. Less than ten years had passed since Hiroshima and Nagasaki. Oh, they were indignant and they protested, but our concerns with the Russians took precedence. And the scars of World War II hadn't had time to heal, so they didn't get much sympathy.

"Well, time passed and things changed. Haverbrook had been doing medical follow-ups since 1956 on the Marshallese who were exposed. It wasn't until 1964 that thyroid abnormalities appeared in the Ailinginae people, and in the Rongelapese. It took another five years for thyroid problems to appear in those on Utrik. Oh, sure, there were reports of leukemias and of abnormal pregnancies, too, but it was felt that those could not be statistically tied to the exposure from fallout. With thyroid problems, it was different. There was radioactive iodine in the fallout and we knew that women and children were more apt to pick up the iodine. Thyroid nodules and cancer were the only things we could definitely say were due to exposure. Anyway, once we discovered cases in the Ailinginae people who had been on Illetto, almost ten years had gone by since Bravo. The Marshallese were already angry, not only about being moved off Rongelap but also because of our bases on Kwajalein and Roi-Namur. Their living conditions on Ebeye and Mejato, as you know, were not ideal. To raise the issue of Illetto at that point would have exacerbated the problems. So we decided to simply include those who had been on Illetto with the people of Ailinginae."

"Yes," protested Jodi. "But people then went to live permanently on Illetto. How do we know that the land and the water around the island aren't contaminated? Were studies done to see if the food grown on Illetto is contaminated or if the fish are affected?"

"If those studies were done, I'm not privy to the results. Some of the information is still classified as top secret. There is one thing I do know and this information must not leave this room. A decision was made at that time by our military. Illetto provided a good opportunity to see what happened to people who continued to live in a contaminated zone. The findings could then be compared with those in people who were evacuated from exposed islands after the blast."

For several moments, Jodi was speechless. "My God!" she finally blurted out. "You're telling me we're using a group of people as guinea pigs without their permission."

"To say anything now, Doctor Larsen, would be counter-productive. Our relations with the Marshallese, as you know, have worsened. They know that the money flowing in from Uncle Sam will not continue indefinitely. And even though they are a sovereign republic, they know that the United States has no intention of giving up its bases on Kwajalein and Roi-Namur. The Marshallese have a lot of ocean but only seventy square miles of land. Their population keeps growing and their little islands simply can't accomodate it. Look at Ebeye. Thirteen thousand people on ninety-three acres. It's a tinder box. And these days people pay attention to what the Japanese say. Many people throughout the world support them in their anti-nuclear stance. The Japanese medical team that was invited here recently by the Marshallese claims that the Americans have been engaged in a coverup, that there is much more contamination than our studies show, and many more potentially serious medical problems. That places the United States in a difficult spot."

"Are you saying our military priorities, our bases here, are more important than people?"

"I'm not saying anything. I'm laying out some facts." The smile was now gone and the anger in Chambers' voice unmistakable.

"And this?" Jodi again pointed to the table, her hand trembling in agitation. "How do we explain this monstrosity? What if genetic changes are happening in the people on the island from eating the breadfruit and crabs and fish?"

"All good questions," said Chambers, her voice calmer. "And you're right. The most important thing right now is not politics but this monstrosity, as you call it. I have an idea who can help us. I have to put a call in to the U.S. to see if I can reach him. You've checked in at the lodge, haven't you?"

"No, I came directly here from the airport."

"Why don't you check in then, rent yourself a bike and get something to eat at the snackbar. It may take a while to reach the person I have to call. Please don't tell anyone why you came. Make up something . . . to pick up supplies, whatever. I'll get these things stowed away on ice. Let's plan to meet at the club at seven. We can have a drink, get some dinner and talk some more. I hope to have some information for you by then." The rigid smile was back in place.

As Jodi stood to leave, Chambers began placing the arm and head back into the plastic trash disposal bag Jodi had brought them in. "Do you need a ride to the lodge?" she asked.

"I'll walk," Jodi said, still troubled by their conversation.

"See you at seven then. And Doctor Larsen," Chambers called, as Jodi started out the door. "Thanks again. For flying this in. And for your discretion."

Jodi closed the door behind her and left the hospital quickly, hoping to avoid anyone she knew. A breeze was coming off the water along Ocean Road and the sky was beginning to darken. Heedless of the humid heat, she walked at a brisk pace, hoping she could make it to the lodge without getting drenched in one of Kwajalein's brief, heavy showers. But the threatening black clouds did not open up until Jodi was at the front desk, checking in and arranging her bicycle rental.

Lying on her bed in Kwaj Lodge, the island's quarters for short-stay visitors, Jodi stared at the ceiling and listened to the drumming of the rain on her window which faced the ocean. The palm trees behind the lodge, lashed by the winds coming off the Pacific, swayed as their fronds stretched out in a westerly direction. Virginia Chambers' words, "a good opportunity to see what happened to people who continued to live in a contaminated zone," played over and over in her mind like a defective CD while the image of the almost human upper extremity and the dolphin-like head with human eyes burned in her memory.

Doctor Chambers had said she counted on Jodi's discretion, but Jodi felt under no obligation to Chambers or to the Department of Energy. Still, to whom could she speak about Mero Attri's find? And Chambers could always deny having told Jodi anything. Perhaps it would be best to simply wait and see what Chambers had in mind when she mentioned someone who might be able to help. Exhausted, Jodi closed her eyes and slept deeply.

She was awakened by the phone ringing on the table next to her bed. For a few seconds, Jodi could not remember where she was. Then she quickly reached for the receiver and heard Doctor Chambers' voice. "Doctor Larsen, I finally reached the person I spoke to you about. Can you meet me a little earlier, let's say at six? I'll be at the bar in the club."

Jodi looked at her watch. It was almost five. "I'll be there," she said.

She took a quick shower, then picked out her bicycle at the rack in front of the lodge. The rain had now ended and been replaced by late afternoon sunshine and high patchy clouds. Kwajalein's flat terrain and small size, little more than a square mile in area, made bicycling an ideal way to get around. The few vehicles on the island, all marked with a USAKA logo, belonged to the military. The roads belonged mostly to cyclists and pedestrians willing to brave the heat.

Jodi vividly remembered how she had arrived in the Marshalls more than a year ago. After hours of seeing nothing but ocean and clouds, the plane had approached a coral reef formation. The islands in the atoll, named after Kwajalein, the largest, were strung out like pearls in a necklace, each surrounded by a turquoise setting. The atoll formed a crescent loop that enclosed the biggest lagoon in the world, almost a thousand square miles. A large part of that lagoon, the so-called mid-atoll corridor, was used as a target area for missiles fired from California's Vandenberg Air Force Base.

Landing on Kwajalein, its runway stretching out along the sea, was like being deposited on a miniscule piece of America set in the middle of the Pacific Ocean. Directly opposite the small terminal, Jodi had spotted the lodge and a church. Only a short walk from there were baseball fields, an outdoor movie theatre and tennis courts. Most of the buildings in the airport's vicinity were no different from those on any American base. But instead of the military personnel Jodi expected, the majority of Americans on the island were civilians manning the missile and radar stations. Bicycling north from the lodge along Ocean Road, Jodi had encountered an intersecting street that was the downtown focus of the island, a street with a bank, a snack bar, a department store called Macy's and a Ten-Ten Supermarket. An American post office was located in the immediate vicinity.

Running parallel to Ocean Road was another main thoroughfare, Lagoon Road, lined with small homes and immaculate lawns, a Pacific suburbia. Blond, suntanned children played in the street and rode their bicycles. She had passed another supermarket, this one named Surfway, a children's playground, a high school, and eventually came to Emon beach where Americans lounged in the sun or snorkeled in the calm waters enclosed by the reef. The only Marshallese she had seen were clerks in the stores or men performing manual labor. It was not what she had anticipated.

A few days later she had taken the ferry, an old American landing craft, to Ebeye, the island where she was scheduled to work for her first year and from which the Marshallese working on Kwajalein commuted daily. Although only a short half-hour from Kwajalein, the two islands were poles apart. Thousands of people lived in houses of cinder block, cement, plywood and aluminum. The waters of the harbor had been filled with floating debris—plastic containers, soda cans and raw sewage. A slick of oil coated the surface. The new hospital where Jodi had expected to work had never been completed. Having run out of money, the Marshallese had simply terminated construction. The hospital being used was only twenty years old but had not fared well in its exposure to the tropical climate and to the desperate poverty. Plaster crumbled from the walls, light fixtures had been ripped out and equipment looted. Often there had been no water or electricity. Most of the island's population had been uprooted from Kwajalein when the American base had been built. Some had been fortunate enough to find jobs on Kwajalein, but the majority were unemployed.

Eventually, Jodi had accustomed herself to Ebeye, just as she had become inured to the deprivations of Malawi during her Peace Corps days. But whenever she had taken the ferry back to Kwajalein, she had found it difficult to suppress the anger surging within her.

And now that she was once again on this sanitized strip of Kwajalein, that same anger boiled within her, intensified by what Virginia Chambers had said.

It was still too early to meet Doctor Chambers so Jodi bicycled past the small hospital only one block from downtown and luxurious compared to Ebeye's. She headed for the turnoff that led to the northern tip of the island where she sat on a bench perched above the water line and watched the surf breaking on the distant reef. To the west she could make out the ferry making its run back to Ebeye and beyond the reef to the east, a fishing boat bobbing on the gentle waves.

She suddenly thought of Mero Attri and wondered how affected he had been by his strange experience. She doubted he would tell anyone. Even if he were to inadvertently mention his find, who would believe him? She found herself feeling sorry for him.

She had left Illetto so quickly that she had not had time to tell anyone. She had left a hurried note on the clinic door saying she would be back in a few days. The fisherman might think her sudden disappearance had something to do with his find, but the other islanders would simply think she had some business on Kwajalein. She found herself now longing for Illetto. From the very first moment of her arrival there, she had been comfortable in that island's remote, tranquil setting. No ersatz America there. No third world squalor. It was what she had expected the Marshalls to be.

Jodi looked down at her watch. It was almost six. She quickly pedalled over to Ocean Road and headed for the club. Dusk was just settling over the island and the street lights were now on. To her left the ocean continued its ceaseless roll and she noticed plovers tracking their way across the sand. During her first days on Kwajalein she had walked that beach many times, picking up fragments of pink coral and shells.

She left her bicycle among at least thirty others in front of the Yokwe Yuk Club. After five o'clock, when the bar opened, the club became a hub of social activity. It was where the Americans went not only to eat or drink but also to dance, to play the arcade games, to feel somehow more immersed in America.

From the entrance hall Jodi turned left into the bar. It was still early and the dance floor was dark as was the DJ's booth, from which music would blare as the evening wore on. Most of the seats at the bar were already filled, the people talking loudly among themselves or watching the Armed Forces Radio and Television Network news on the screen above the bar. Alcohol was the one inexpensive commodity here and the Americans, mostly single and lonely, sought solace in it.

All heads now turned to Jodi as the men were suddenly aware of her presence.

The tables were cloaked in the same darkness as the dance floor and Jodi walked among them looking for Virginia Chambers. She found her hidden in the shadows at a table in the far corner. Chambers sat stiffly, staring at her drink, unaware of Jodi's approach. The strange expression on her face made Jodi apprehensive.

"Hello. Is everything all right?"

Startled, Virginia Chambers blinked. "Oh, yes, I didn't see you come in. Sit down, please."

The waitress, a young Filipino woman, came over and Jodi ordered a glass of wine.

"I was thinking about my dog," said Doctor Chambers. "She's a samoyed. I've had her for a long time. I miss her."

"Where is she now?"

"With my sister in Cambridge. Do you have any pets?"

"No, I don't."

"I've had Trixie for ten years. She's a wonderful companion. Helps to fend off loneliness, you know."

Jodi was surprised at the older woman's candor and wondered if she had had too much to drink, a thought quickly dispelled when Doctor Chambers signalled to the waitress. "I'll have another Coke please."

"Do you have any children?" Jodi asked.

"No, just Trixie. And you? Any husband, children?"

Jodi shook her head as Chambers' rigid smile reappeared.

"Well, I suppose you're anxious to know what I found out."

"Yes, I am."

"His name is James Newell. He's a specialist in internal medicine but better known for his research in genetic diseases. Currently he's at the University of California Hospital in La Jolla. Doctor Newell has been out here with the Haverbrook team several times in the past ten years. I met him during his last visit two years ago."

"You told him about the . . . the fisherman's find?"

"Enough to pique his interest."

"And?"

"He's catching a flight out tomorrow. If he can make his connections he should be here by Friday."

"But that's three days away. I have to get back."

"Not a problem. You can head back tomorrow."

"I don't understand. I'd like to meet him and hear his ideas."

"Oh, you'll meet him all right, but on Illetto."

"He'll come to the island?"

"You can count on it. Newell is an experienced scuba diver. He's been out on some Scripps Oceanographic Institute trips. Once he sees what you brought, I don't think anything would keep him from Illetto."

Jodi could hardly suppress her excitement. "Genetic diseases and scuba diving. He may be just the . . . "

"That's why he was the first person I thought of. You should know that he worked with hibakusha, the radiation survivors from Hiroshima and Nagasaki."

"I can't wait to meet him," Jodi said. "I hope he can help us get to the bottom of this."

"If he doesn't, it won't be for lack of trying. So," she leaned back in her chair, "I'll make your flight arrangements for Roi-Namur and Bikini for tomorrow. The launch from Bikini should have you back on Illetto by tomorrow afternoon." She looked at her watch. "Let's head to the dining room."

FOUR

It was almost midnight when Jim Newell arrived home from a two-day seminar at Stanford Medical School. He was tired from the long drive back to La Jolla and looked forward to a hot shower and bed. But he was almost too excited to think about sleep.

The scientists at Stanford had reported on inherited genetic damage in the population exposed to fallout from the Chernobyl disaster. Children born in 1994 to parents who lived in the areas of Belarus most severely polluted by the meltdown of the reactor in 1986 had been found to have more mutations than expected, mutations that were believed to have been passed on because of changes in the DNA of sperm and eggs. These so-called germline mutations, inherited from the children's parents, had never been reported before, not even in the survivors of Hiroshima and Nagasaki.

The phone rang as he peeled off his clothes. He immediately recognized the clipped speech of Virginia Chambers.

"What a surprise," he said. "Don't tell me you folks at Haverbrook work until the wee hours of the morning."

"I'm calling from Kwaj," she replied. "I have some news that might interest you."

Jim sat down on his bed. He could tell from the guarded tone in her voice that she worried about this call being monitored.

"I've got the parts on ice but I don't know how long I can keep the lid on. If this gets out, we'll have a media circus here."

He was suddenly aware of his rapid heart beat as he listened. "Virginia, I'll rearrange my schedule first thing in the morning. The next Continental Micronesia flight probably isn't until Friday but I'll be on it. Try your best not to let any of this leak out."

"I'll padlock the lab if I have to. Look forward to your arrival."

After the click, he held the phone for several seconds, listening to the silence. Slowly, deeply immersed in his thoughts, he replaced the receiver.

He then showered quickly, crawled into bed and set his alarm for six. His body craved sleep but his eyes refused to cooperate. Chambers' news, following so quickly the information reported at Stanford, was beyond coincidence. It was as if a light had gone on, beckoning him to follow. The possibility of inherited mutations from radioactive fallout was something he had always believed, in spite of the skepticism of many scientists.

It was more than just academic interest to Jim Newell. His mother-in-law, Mitsuo Tanaka, had been a radiation survivor, living in Hiroshima when the first atomic bomb was exploded. Assailed now by memories, first of Mitsuo and then of his beautiful Aiko, he knew sleep would not come easily.

He had met Aiko during his internal medicine residency in Palo Alto in 1976. It was as if it had occurred only yesterday. A woman having an insulin reaction had been brought to the emergency room. On call that night, he had been summoned. The patient was unconscious but he had obtained information from her friend, a young Japanese woman who had driven her to the hospital.

His diabetic patient revived almost immediately after treatment but he kept her there a while, not only to be sure she was fully recovered, but also so he could talk to her friend.

Aiko had come to the United States to attend college and then gone on to Stanford Law School. She was now an instructor in environmental law there. It quickly became apparent that his interest in Aiko was reciprocated. By the time the two women left the hospital, Jim Newell had a dinner date for later that week.

It was a first love for both, so intense that all implications of different cultural backgrounds were swept away. Six months later he married Aiko in Syracuse, New York, Jim's hometown, where his parents still lived and worked as schoolteachers. It was a small wedding attended only by his immediate family. Aiko captivated not only Jim's parents but also his brother and sister. All that marred the landscape of what was the happiest day of Jim Newell's life was the absence of Aiko's family. Her father had died recently from stomach cancer and Aiko's mother, still living in Hiroshima, was ill with leukemia. Aiko was an only child.

They went to Japan for their honeymoon but because of their work schedules, the trip was a whirlwind. Except for a few days in Kyoto, they had spent the remainder of the time in Hiroshima so Aiko could be with her mother.

Mitsuo Tanaka was a gracious, gentle woman. She spoke little English but her warm acceptance of her foreign son-in-law was apparent. She had only recently been released from the hospital and was quite weak. Aiko tried to convince her mother to return to America with them but the woman refused.

"She says she cannot leave her home and her friends," translated Aiko. "She was born here and wants to die here so her ashes can rest in Japanese soil next to my father's."

Hiroshima was an industrial city with little to recommend it for the tourist—except for the evidence of the one moment in its history when it had been obliterated. For long, silent minutes, he and Aiko had stood in front of the ruin of the Industrial Promotion Hall, the building above which the atomic bomb had been detonated. From there they had gone to the nearby Peace Memorial Museum where they poured over the photographed effects of the nuclear blast. Aiko, in spite of having been to the museum before, cried, and he himself had choked back tears. The area around the hall had been converted into a park with a canal that flowed gently through the grounds. He and Aiko bought picnic lunches, then rented a rowboat and drifted on the canal. It was a tranquil ending to a bittersweet day.

When not with Mitsuo, they had spent the remainder of their week riding the tram around the city and visiting shrines on beautiful Miyajima Island, a ten-minute ferry ride from the mainland.

Parting from Mitsuo was difficult. Aiko knew it was probably the last time she would see her mother. She and Jim had spoken to the doctors and been informed that the outlook was dim. Only three weeks after their return to California, Mitsuo had died.

He and Aiko had named the first of their two daughters, born a year after their marriage, Jillian Mitsuo. The second child, Meredith, was born a year later.

Following the completion of his residency and a fellowship in genetic diseases, provoked by his interest in radiation effects on genetic material, he and Aiko had moved to La Jolla. There, Jim had a faculty position in the medical school and Aiko taught at University of San Diego Law School. Their careers prospered and they both received tenured professorships.

Their daughters thrived, each of them following their father's love for water sports. But in 1990, just before the Christmas holidays, the family's happy idyll came to an end.

Aiko developed bleeding from her gums and nose and became anemic. Jim, hoping his suspicions were wrong, prepared a blood smear. Hunched over his microscope, he stared at the pallid red cells and abnormal white blood cells that filled every field. Aiko sat at his side watching intently but she did not speak. Jim looked up, his eyes meeting hers. "I have it, don't I?" she said softly, taking his hands in hers as if he were the one who needed to be consoled.

The oncologists at the university hospital confirmed his diagnosis: acute lymphoblastic leukemia. They explained the treatment protocol and admitted Aiko to the hospital. Jim and the children sat at her bedside the evening of her admission. The girls, unaware of the seriousness of her illness, chattered happily about their upcoming holidays. Aiko laughed with them, but each time she glanced at her husband he could see the concern in her eyes, concern he knew was not for her, but for him. "Take care of your daddy," she said to the girls as they kissed goodbye. That night, the night before she was to receive her first treatment, Aiko died from a massive brain hemorrhage.

Jim was shattered. It was impossible to face life without Aiko. He tried to provide what comfort he could to his daughters, but knew his efforts to help them cope with the loss of their mother were impeded by his own terrible grief. In the end, it was only their love for one another that helped them through those first difficult weeks. Jill and Meredith, only thirteen and twelve at that time, not only returned to school immediately after the holidays but, as if heeding their mother's words, took over the household with a competence that belied their youth.

Jim immersed himself in research. It had long been known that people exposed to excessive amounts of radiation were at increased risk for leukemia. Studies on the survivors of Hiroshima and Nagasaki confirmed this, with the first cases of leukemia appearing two years after the atomic blasts and reaching a peak after five to seven years.

But Mitsuo, his mother-in-law, had developed leukemia, the same type as Aiko's, almost thirty years after the bomb. Even her Japanese physicians were unwilling to ascribe the disease to the effects of the radiation, although they would concede the possibility of chromosome damage. He wondered what those same physicians would say now if they knew about Mitsuo's daughter. They would probably mention the genetic predisposition that exists in some cases of acute leukemia, the fact that if one identical twin, for instance, develops the disease, the other is at increased risk. But would any of them have been willing to consider the possibility of inherited genetic damage? Probably not, or at least, not until now.

The research coming out of the Chernobyl accident certainly showed that such a possibility was more than likely. Until the recent reports, the only health problem blamed with certainty on the radiation from this event was an increase in the cases of thyroid cancer in children living near the power plant. Just as in those exposed to the Bikini blast in the Marshall Islands, that was to be expected because of the radioactive iodine in the emissions. The thyroid gland in children was much more apt to pick up the radioactive element. But there were other radioactive isotopes in the emissions, isotopes such as cesium. A person's cells, apparently, were unable to distinguish cesium from potassium, an essential nutrient. When cells picked up cesium, that isotope became a source of internal radiation.

If the reports from Chernobyl were correct, if genetic damage was inherited, what did that mean for Jill and Meredith? Were they likely to be at increased risk for leukemia? And if so, what could he do about it? It was that thought, more than any other, that drove Jim Newell in his research.

After the data he had heard during the Stanford seminar, the phone call from Virginia Chambers was like adding gasoline to a burning fire.

Flight reservations were no problem. He would be on a plane from San Diego to Honolulu that afternoon. He then spoke to Doctor Chambers' secretary at Haverbrook. She arranged the Continental Micronesia leg of his trip for Friday morning, the tickets to be delivered to him at his hotel in Honolulu. She agreed to leave his return date open.

He then called Jillian and Meredith to let them know. Jill was now in her second year at Stanford and Meredith was a freshman at University of California in Santa Cruz. Both were surprised by his sudden trip to Kwajalein and their father's vague answers to their questions only prompted more curiosity. "I know you're hiding something, Dad," Jill said, perceptive as always. "It certainly sounds mysterious," added Meredith, more subtly. Chuckling at how well they knew him, he promised more information when they returned home during their spring break, three weeks away.

"I'm sure I'll be back by then," he said, "but if there's any delay, I'll call you from Kwaj."

He then started packing his scuba gear and clothes. Standard for the Marshalls, because of the heat and humidity, were shorts and teeshirts. They took only moments to collect. But Newell was particular about his diving gear. He arranged his mask, snorkel, fins, spear gun and knife, regulator, BCD, weight belt and gauges on the bed, then packed them in a separate duffel bag. The last items were an underwater camera and rolls of film. He knew he could obtain scuba tanks and most of the gear he was carrying on Kwajalein, but using gear he was accustomed to, gear that he had cleaned and maintained, provided a feeling of security.

Jim got to the hospital before eight and met with colleagues in his department. He arranged replacements for his lectures and fended questions about the suddeness of the trip, telling them only that his presence in the Marshalls had been requested by the Department of Energy. "But I might have an interesting story for you when I get back," he offered, sounding deliberately mysterious.

In a hurriedly arranged meeting with the hospital administrator and medical director, Jim Newell disclosed a few rudimentary details. He was purposefully vague about the fisherman's find, describing it simply as a mutant life form.

"Do you think there's a radiation tie-in?" asked Doctor Knowles, the medical director.

"Key question, Ralph. I hope I'll have some answers by the time I get back. If I have anything to report before, I'll call you from Kwaj. And if you need to reach me, here's Doctor Chambers' office phone number at Haverbrook. Her secretary will get any messages to me."

Newell then conducted abbreviated rounds with the students, his thoughts already thousands of miles away. Ordinarily patient with the students, he found himself glancing frequently at his watch and giving uncharacteristically curt replies to their questions. Noticing the puzzled looks, he apologized, explaining that he had to leave early for the airport.

Jim arrived at San Diego's Lindbergh Field with minutes to spare and it was only when the 747 lifted off that he was able to relax. As the California coastline receded in the distance, Jim closed his eyes. Exhausted from a sleepless night and the runaway thoughts prompted by Virginia Chambers' phone call, he slept soundly, awakening only when the flight attendant touched his shoulder and asked him to put his seat in the upright position for landing. Glancing out the window, he was surprised to see the highrises of Honolulu with the lush hillsides of Oahu behind them.

Immediately after checking into the Outrigger East in Waikiki, he telephoned John Carmody, a radiologist at Tripler Army Hospital, with whom he had worked in Kwajalein two years earlier. Like Newell, Carmody had a particular interest in the effects of nuclear radiation.

The following morning, the two men met in Tripler's library. This time, Newell said nothing about any mutant forms. But he did talk about the seminar he had attended at Stanford and pumped Carmody for information on any recent reports he might have run across in the medical literature that dealt with long-term radiation damage. "I try to keep abreast of everything that comes out," he explained, "but wanted to make sure I hadn't overlooked anything in radiologic journals." Carmody had nothing to add. After Chernobyl, there were the usual conflicting reports on birth defects and miscarriages. Not enough time had passed to see if the chromosome damage that had occurred would lead to leukemia or other cancers.

Jim knew that studies from the University of Michigan had failed to confirm the presence of germline mutations or DNA changes in sperm and eggs in Japanese atomic bomb survivors and their children, but there were major differences between the Japanese explosions and the Bikini H-Bomb blasts and the Chernobyl accident. H-Bomb Bravo had thirteen hundred times the destructive force of the Hiroshima bomb; fallout radiation was intense in some areas. And in Chernobyl, where the radiation was less intense, it was longer lasting.

Prompted by Jim's questioning, Carmody discussed the DNA areas called minisatellites. "These are more prone to mutations, but they're not functioning genes. If these mutations are passed on from generation to generation, we still don't know if there's any significance. We don't even know the purpose of minisatellites. But I will concede this, Jim. No one can say that inherited genetic damage doesn't occur. You can bet that after these recent reports on germline mutations, we're going to be seeing a lot more studies.

"But now you've aroused my curiosity. Why all this interest in the subject? Does this trip to Kwaj have anything to do with it?"

Jim Newell hated to lie to Carmody, a friend, and he was a fellow physician. But Jim couldn't ignore the fact that Carmody was a U.S. Army major, and it was this military affiliation that gave him pause.

"I was mainly interested because of my wife and her mother having had leukemia. My mother-in-law, I believe I told you, had been at Hiroshima when the bomb was exploded." And, thought Jim, my interest on that account is not a lie.

"Well," said Carmody. "I'm sorry I couldn't come up with some pearls that might have been of interest to you. Listen, you have a good stay on Kwaj and give my regards to Chambers." He laughed, as if suddenly remembering something. "She's one tough cookie, isn't she? If I spot anything new in the literature, I'll send copies to La Jolla."

On Friday, Jim began island hopping to Kwajalein, with stops on Johnston Island, another American base two hours from Honolulu, and Majuro, the capital of the Republic of the Marshall Islands. Majuro, which Newell had visited briefly during a previous trip to Kwajalein, was, like Ebeye, another overpopulated island, with as many as thirty-six hundred people per square mile.

Soon the crescent shape of Kwajalein, half the island seemingly taken up by the airfield's runway, appeared outside his window. Stepping out of the small terminal on Kwajalein, Newell couldn't believe two years had gone by since his last visit. Nothing had changed. The enervating heat had him sweating in a matter of minutes. He glanced up at the American and Marshallese flags stretched out in a westward direction by the trade winds coming off the ocean. Between them was a small monument commemorating the World War II battle for the island and off to one side an artillery piece pointing out to sea.

A nearby signpost indicated that Kwajalein was twenty-one hundred miles from Honolulu, thirty-one hundred sixty miles from Hong Kong and seventy-one hundred fifty-six miles from Washington, DC. The middle of nowhere, thought Newell, as he hefted his bags across the street to the lodge.

After checking in and getting a bicycle, he pedalled along Ocean Road under overcast skies to the hospital. Virginia Chambers was waiting.

"Good to see you, Doctor Newell," she said, extending her hand. "I really appreciate your coming out on such short notice."

Jim had noticed while working with her during his last stay on the island that she used a formal address with everyone, even those she had known for some time.

As comfortable as Doctor Chambers was with formality, Jim was not. "Nice to see you, Virginia," he said. "I saw John Carmody while I was in Honolulu and he sends you his best."

"Well, no sense wasting time," she replied. Let's go to the lab."

Her aversion to small talk made Jim suppress a smile as he followed. She was exactly as he remembered her. 'One tough cookie,' as John Carmody had put it. They walked through the main laboratory to a small room in the rear and closed the door. He immediately noticed the padlock on the large refrigerator.

"Hasn't anyone asked you about that?"

"Oh, I just tell them I keep valuable supplies in there."

She removed a bulky plastic sack from the refrigerator and placed it on the table. Newell felt his excitement mounting as Chambers gingerly retrieved the contents. They had become somewhat dessicated after several days in the cold but all details were still clearly visible.

Jim sat down at the table and lifted the arm. He realized it was much like any human arm except for the absence of fingernails and the webbing between the fingers. The skin, chalky white in color and with a parchment-like consistency, was covered with a soft, down-like hair, the type that covered a human fetus and persisted after birth. Frozen strands of torn muscle hung from the end.

He carefully put it down and turned to the grey-colored head. It resembled that of a bottle-nosed dolphin, a type commonly found in the Pacific, but the snout was much blunter, its rounded appearance more like a porpoise. He noted that the blowhole was close to the mouth rather than high in the head. The eyes were like no eyes he had ever seen in a sea mammal. Even with the glazed appearance of death, they were clearly human eyes with coarse lashes. Along the lower lateral sides of the head were the remnants of a visceral arch but no real gill apparatus.

Newell turned the head and stared directly into its face. He couldn't decide whether it looked like a dolphin with humanoid attributes or a human with cetacean tendencies. He gingerly pried open the mouth. The tongue, like the lips, was absent. More like a dolphin there, he thought.

He turned to Doctor Chambers, who had watched intently during his examination. "Have you taken any X-Rays?"

"I couldn't very well do that without everyone finding out."

"Maybe tonight we can go down to radiology and do it ourselves. A pity we don't have the rest of the body."

"Any ideas so far?"

"What can I say? At first glance it's like looking at the parts of two separate entities. If it wasn't for the webbing between the fingers and the absence of nails, I'd be inclined to wonder if the fisherman's boat hit both a person and some sort of sea creature. But I don't think so. Assuming these parts come from the same organism, I'd have to say it's a true mammal but one somewhere between a sea and land mammal. The features of the face, especially the eyes and the position of the blowhole, and the arm, almost human, seem to indicate that it was a land mammal in the not too distant past, one that's been gradually metamorphosing into a sea mammal. It took our present-day dolphins millions of years to make that transition."

He pointed at the visceral arch. "If you remember your embryology, you know these visceral arches occur in human embryos up to about seven weeks. All vertebrate embryos in their early development go through a stage where they resemble one another."

"The embryo's development repeats the history of the race," said Chambers.

"Right. What we all learned as ontogeny recapitulates phylogeny. In this creature, the arch persisted but there is no gill apparatus."

"There's no way to make an educated guess as to when the first of these creatures might have appeared?"

Newell raised his hand. "You're getting ahead of yourself, Virginia. We don't know if there are other creatures like this."

"My guess is that if there's one, there have to be others. Every mammal has parents, you know. We may never be able to prove it, but I feel Bravo has played a role in this."

"I have no argument with anything you say but we need proof. Who's the doctor who brought these?"

"Jodi Larsen with the Public Health Service. She worked on Ebeye for a year and is now on Illetto."

"So, to recap what you told me, a fisherman from that island ran over this—whatever it is—then retrieved the pieces from the water and took them to this Doctor Larsen. She then brought them to you."

"Yes. And she also suspects radiation from Bravo is responsible. She found out from some of the elders on the island that there were Marshallese on Illetto during the Bravo detonation. Some of those people are still on Illetto and others are in Ailinginae where they were from originally. The people on Illetto don't want anything said to their own government because they're afraid they'll be evacuated. As you can imagine, the Marshallese government would love an issue like this to keep American dollars flowing. Doctor Larsen was very upset when I told her we've known for more than thirty years that people had been on Illetto during Bravo and that our scientists were willing to let them stay there to see the effects of long-term exposure."

"Is that true?"

"About our scientists? Let's just say I can't give you names but it is true."

"I can't blame Larsen for getting upset. That behavior is unconscionable."

"I agree. But they would deny it."

Jim took a deep breath, thought for a moment and then said, "I'd like to go out to Illetto."

"I thought so. You're already booked on tomorrow morning's flight to Roi-Namur and Bikini. Our Bikini people will then take you to Illetto by boat."

He smiled. "You haven't changed, Virginia. As efficient as always."

"So, we'll try to X-Ray them tonight, and then? Do you want me to keep them locked up or ship them back to the States?"

"Keep them here. Locked up. How do I get in touch with you from Illetto?"

"Doctor Larsen has a radio. Well then, I'll have you picked up at the lodge at eight tomorrow morning."

Chambers stored the specimens back in the freezer and replaced the padlock to the door.

"Good luck," she said, her hand extended, as they parted outside the hospital. "I hope you find some answers for us."

"It's a big ocean, but maybe we'll get lucky. See you," he called, waving from his bicycle. He crossed Ocean Road and stopped near the beach, then sat on a bench to watch the water and gather his thoughts. The tide was in and the surf rolled over the sand, exposing and removing bits of coral and shell. This same water, he thought, was rolling off the shores of Illetto. He wondered what he would find beneath its surface.

FIVE

Jodi Larsen had expected him. But when a tall, slender American wearing khaki shirt and shorts appeared in the clinic doorway, she was frankly surprised.

"Hi. You must be Doctor Larsen. I'm Jim Newell."

Slightly embarrassed, she extended her hand. "Jodi Larsen. Doctor Chambers said you'd be coming, but suddenly seeing someone who wasn't Marshallese startled me."

"So this is where you work," Jim said, walking around the room, hoping to put her at ease. "Just your typical stateside office." He ran his hand across the coarsely woven mat that covered the examination table and smiled at her.

"I've worked in worse," said Jodi. "Have you been to Ebeye?"

"Ah, yes, Ebeye. The flower of the Marshalls. One of the fringe benefits of American trusteeship."

"Do I detect a cynic?" Jodi asked with feigned surprise.

"Well, I try not to be, but sometimes it just sneaks out. No patients this afternoon?"

"It's slow today. I usually walk around the island in the morning making housecalls then head over here every so often to see if any patients are waiting. If there's an emergency I'm not difficult to find since the island is so small."

"What are the major health problems on Illetto?"

"The same as on Ebeye—diabetes, high blood pressure, obesity—but not to the same extent. The people here, or half of them at least, still eat traditional foods. And, of course, I see some infectious disease and minor trauma—diarrheas, cuts, sprains—no fractures yet, thank goodness." Jodi rapped her knuckles on the wooden table. "Would you like me to show you around the island? It's quite pretty. And then I'll take you to where you'll be staying. Where are your bags?"

"There was a house near that old dock where the boat dropped me off. The woman there said I could leave the bags. Or at least that's what I think she said. She didn't speak English."

"That must be Mero Attri's wife. Mero is the one who accidentally killed the . . . you know," she added softly.

"He's the man I want to meet then."

"You didn't see a boat at the dock?"

"No."

"He must be out fishing. That's a long day for him. The fishing is still fairly good here, not like down near Kwaj, where the Japanese and Chinese have depleted it. They tend to stay away from here."

"Too close to Bikini and Enewetak?"

"That's my guess. The Japanese, you know, still feel the U.S. isn't telling the truth about contamination of the sea life. They've had their own scientific teams in the Marshalls by invitation of the Marshallese government."

Jodi and Jim Newell then headed for the beach.

"This is where I first saw those things. Mero had pulled his boat up on the sand and was just sitting there. I think he was in shock and I could understand why. Did Doctor Chambers show you those parts?"

Jim nodded. "Do you think the fisherman could take us out to where it happened?"

"I don't know. The Marshallese are superstitious. He thinks because he broke a taboo by taking his wife out fishing someone put the evil eye on him. We'll ask. You're a diver, I understand."

"Yes. I have my gear with me."

"Where will you get your tanks?"

"The fellows at Bikini station gave me four. They're with my bags."

As they strolled along the beach, plovers and sand crabs scurried in front of them along the surf's edge while petrels hovered above the water in the distance.

"It's a beautiful beach," said Newell.

"Yes," Jodi agreed. "I come down every morning for a swim." She motioned to a path cutting through the coconut palms. "We can head up this way. It'll take us to the one store on the island. Lekoj Kel, the owner, has two homes there. He uses one for family members visiting from Ailinginae. That's where you'll be staying. After you meet Kel, we'll come back to get your things."

Two boys drinking bottles of warm Coca Cola were just coming out of the store as Jodi and Newell approached.

"Whatever happened to coconut milk?" Jim asked.

"Unfortunately," said Jodi, laughing, "Coke is tough competition."

Recognizing Jodi, Kel came from behind the counter and Jodi introduced the two men. They shook hands. Kel's English was rudimentary so Jodi translated.

"I'm impressed," said Jim. "Your Marshallese sounds flawless."

"I'm blessed with a facility for languages. When I go home for a visit, it will probably make me the only Marshallese language speaker in New Hampshire."

Jim laughed. "You'll have to talk to yourself to keep in practice."

Kel took them around to the hut behind the store. Wooden crates served as chairs and a table. There were several woven palm carpets on the ground, but nothing else.

"Were you warned to bring a cot?" Jodi asked.

"No, but that's all right. The carpets will be fine."

"Sleeping on the ground was one thing I couldn't get used to," said Jodi. "That's probably because when I worked in Africa I was afraid of snakes. So I always carry a fold-up cot with me."

"What do you do for a pillow? I think I'll miss that."

Jodi laughed. "I can thank Continental Micronesia for the pillow I took from the plane."

"Thanks for arranging the accomodations," said Jim, as they headed for Mero Attri's house.

"Nothing but the best for a distinguished visitor."

"I don't know about that distinguished part."

"Doctor Chambers speaks highly of you." She threw a quick glance at Newell. "She thinks you can provide some answers."

"I appreciate her confidence in me, but . . . " He turned to Jodi. "No guarantees. She understands that."

Mero Attri and his wife, nursing the new baby, were sitting in front of their home. Their sons were engaged in a wrestling match. Jodi spotted Jim Newell's suitcases and scuba tanks at the side of the hut. Mero stood up as they approached and Jodi introduced him. They all sat down on the sandy ground and Mero's wife took the baby inside, calling the two boys to follow her.

Jodi explained why Jim was on the island and told him that Doctor Newell wanted to take a look at the area where the accident had happened. Mero would be paid for his time.

Jim, not understanding the conversation, looked from one to the other, then at the fishing boat on the sand near the dock. Mero was unsettled by what Jodi was asking and kept his eyes to the ground. He nervously picked up handfuls of sand, staring at the streams of sand flowing between his fingers. Jodi spoke softly, an earnest look on her face, hoping to break down any resistance. Finally, he nodded slowly.

Jodi turned to Jim. "Well, he's not thrilled with the idea, as you can probably tell. I told him you'd pay for his time, but it's not a question of money. He's simply afraid to go back there. Anyway, I've convinced him to take us tomorrow at sunrise. You don't mind if I tag along, do you?"

"Of course not. Ask him if I can leave the tanks and diving gear here."

Mero nodded. As Jim rose to leave, Jodi asked Mero one more question. For the first time a smile crossed his face. He quickly went inside and returned with a red snapper that weighed about three pounds. Jodi held the fish as if weighing it and gave him a dollar. "This is dinner," she said to Jim, "and you're invited."

"Terrific." He retrieved a small black canvas duffle bag and followed Jodi back to Kel's store.

"This is a little different from Kwaj," she said, as he deposited his bag in the hut.

"For washing up and bathing, there's the ocean. Your bathroom facilities are . . . " She swung her arm in a wide arc. "Wherever. I'm sure Kel will show you.There's bottled water in the store and, if you want, you can collect rainwater—we get plenty of that. Of course, there's lots of coconut milk. If you get tired of fish, coconut, bananas and breadfruit, Kel keeps canned and packaged goods from America and Japan."

Jodi then pointed to the sun sinking low on the horizon. "Get your swimsuit and grab a towel. We'll have a fast dip and get a fire going for dinner. Oh, bring a flashlight. If you don't have one, I've got an extra."

Newell quickly changed, grabbed a towel and flashlight from his bag, and rejoined Jodi, waiting outside. As they neared her hut, she asked him to cut a bunch of bananas from one of the nearby trees.

"We'll pick up some coconuts for our drinks."

"I like that," said Newell. "Just pick your food off the trees or catch it in the ocean. There aren't too many places left like this."

"I'll let you hold this," she said, handing him the fish.

He followed her into her hut where she busied herself gathering a metal grill, and some utensils, dishes, and wooden matches that she placed in a woven bag. She took a final glance around and picked up a lantern and towel.

"Same deluxe accomodations as mine, I see. But aren't you forgetting something?"

Jodi paused and turned. "What?"

"The bottle of fume blanc. Or at least a chardonnay."

She laughed. "Dream on."

Jim followed her down the path to the beach where they paused at a heap of ashes.

"This is the barbecue pit I've been working on since I arrived."

Jim looked down at the pile of charred coconut fronds and husks with a slight smile.

"Don't laugh," said Jodi. "It's no small accomplishment."

They piled their things on the sand, then stood looking at one another for an instant.

Jim smiled broadly. "What's next, scoutleader?"

"A swim," said Jodi, darting toward the water.

Plunging through the surf, they swam out about fifty yards.

"This is quite a perk—a private pool," said Jim breathlessly, treading water.

"I never did this in Lake Winnipesaukee in March," said Jodi, coming closer.

They floated on their backs, watching the first stars appear between the clouds.

"We'd better head back and get that dinner started," called Jodi as she headed for shore.

Dusk descended rapidly as the sun plunged into the ocean, silhouetting the palm trees against a deepening violet sky. They swam with smooth, even strokes, keeping pace with one another. The plovers, startled, darted out of the way as they splashed through the surf.

"How are your fire-making skills?" Jodi asked as they dried themselves on the beach.

"I never did make Eagle Scout, but I'll give it a try."

"I'll be back in a minute," said Jodi.

When she returned, Jim had the beginnings of a fire, the dried fronds and husk fibers curling before bursting into flame. Jodi was carrying two coconuts and a machete.

"You really have gone native," he said.

"You're not doing so badly yourself. That's a nice fire."

Jodi moved the grill over the flames and carefully placed the fish on it. She peeled and sliced the bananas onto their plates and hacked the tops off the coconuts. Soon the fish was browned and crisp. "It's not fancy, but we know everything is fresh."

"This is delicious," Jim said as the darkness closed in around them. "And the coconut milk is sweeter than any I've ever had."

"That's why the Marshallese used to come here from Ailinginae. Did Doctor Chambers mention anything about that?"

He nodded. "She told me people were here during the Bravo blast although no one knew about it until years later."

"What else did she tell you?"

"That you were upset about people being used as guinea pigs."

"How do you feel about that?"

"The same as you."

After a few moments of silence Jodi asked "What do you make of Mero Attri's find?"

Jim placed his dish on the sand. "I can give you two answers, one scientific and one a gut feeling."

"I'd like to hear both."

"Scientifically, I have to be honest and say I don't know. There are many questions that have to be answered. Could this be an isolated mutation? And if not, how many such creatures are there? Are they only around Illetto? What does the rest of this creature look like? And most important, were they here before 1954?"

Jodi stared intently at him. "And your gut feeling?"

"Remember," he said, "this is totally unscientific. It's just what I feel. I believe this is related to Bravo. We know radiation can cause chromosome damage and I happen to believe genetic damage can be inherited."

"That was my first thought when Mero showed me what he had hit. I still can't get the images out of my mind."

"I admit to being just as shocked as you were. I'm sure Doctor Chambers was affected the same way. She's walking on eggshells right now, not knowing what to do. If our feelings turn out to be fact, I don't have to tell you what the repercussions can be. Our government . . . "

"I don't care what our government thinks," Jodi flashed. "And I don't care about the politics. Our scientists think they can conduct experiments on people without their knowledge or consent. If our H-Bombs did this . . . . "

Newell held up his hand. "Whoa. I'm not arguing with you. I'm just pointing out that our government will have a real mess on its hands. It's a good example of people who play with fire getting burned."

"Unfortunately, innocent people sometimes get burned, too. I'm sorry. I'm not angry at you. I've just been upset ever since Doctor Chambers told me that our government knew Illetto was contaminated but preferred to do nothing about it."

"You have a right to be upset. It's a completely immoral act."

For a long time there was a strained silence with only the sound of the surf.

"I'm looking forward to our boat ride tomorrow morning," Jim said finally. "I certainly appreciate your convincing—what's his name? Mero? I can understand his reluctance to go back but I don't suppose he'll have any trouble finding it."

"These fishermen are great navigators. You can trust him to get you to the exact spot. Do you know about their stick charts?" Jodi asked.

"No, what's that?"

"Well, the islands here are so flat and so far apart that the earliest settlers learned to travel between them in their canoes by reading the waves. They learned the patterns of different waves and swells and then taught them to their children by making charts of sticks tied together to represent the various formations. It's really quite ingenious."

"I'll say. You've learned a lot in your time here."

"That's one advantage of signing up for two year stints."

"My previous visits were only for a few weeks. I was usually so busy that before I knew it, I was flying back to the States. It never gave me any time for cultural immersion. You and I were almost neighbors back home, you know."

"Really?"

"Well, you're from New Hampshire and I grew up in Syracuse."

"But you're in California now?"

He nodded. "I did most of my medical training in Palo Alto and then moved to the University Hospital in La Jolla. My daughters are both in college in California."

"Is your wife a physician, too?"

Jim was silent for a moment. He had always hated euphemisms like "passed away" but still found it difficult to describe Aiko as dead. Each time he used the word, its finality brought back the pain. "I lost my wife several years ago."

"Oh, I'm so sorry," said Jodi, embarrassed.

"That's really what got me so involved with radiation-induced genetic diseases. My wife was Japanese. Her mother lived in Hiroshima. She died of leukemia and later, my wife did also."

"I can understand now why you're interested in what's happening here. Do you know what came to my mind after I saw what Mero Attri had brought in and then had my talk with Doctor Chambers? It was something Robert Oppenheimer said after the first atomic explosion at Alamogordo. He said 'physicists have known sin and this is a knowledge which they cannot lose.' I have a feeling that if he were alive today, that monstrosity would not have come as a surprise to him."

They stared at the fire, immersed in their own thoughts, until Jim broke the silence.

"Where do you call home these days, Jodi?"

"That's a good question. After I finished my family practice residency, I went into the Peace Corps and spent two years in Malawi. Then I came here with the Public Health Service. I guess at this point home is wherever I happen to be."

"Have you thought about what you'll do when your time here is up?"

"Not really."

"No family responsibilities?"

She shook her head. "No husband, no children, and my parents are still in good health. I've enjoyed the past few years. New places, new cultures, interesting medical problems. The thought of a private family practice makes me shudder."

Jim laughed. "Yes, I can see where that would pale compared to Malawi and the Marshalls."

"Are your daughters planning to go into medicine?"

"If they are they haven't said anything to me. They're both good students but neither has decided on a major yet."

"Would you like them to be physicians?"

"It's funny. You're the first person who's ever asked me that."

"I'm just curious."

"It's a good question. I wouldn't mind, of course, but . . . " Jim stared at the fire, trying to formulate his thoughts. "I know it sounds trite, but I'd just like them to do whatever makes them happy. Did you always know you wanted to be a doctor?"

"As far back as I can remember."

"The same with me."

The fire was dying down and they now sat enveloped in the darkness. Jodi, aware of how comfortable she felt talking to this man whom she had known only a few hours, fidgeted nervously with the plate on her lap.

"Well," she said, quickly standing. "Time to get the dishes done."

Jim followed her to the water's edge where they knelt in the surf and scrubbed their plates. When they returned to the embers, Jodi lit the kerosene lantern.

"We should be at Mero's house at sunrise so we can get an early start," she said. "Do you want me to wake you?"

"I'm an early riser. I'll be up."

"If you get to my place before the sun's up, I'll have coffee made. Just grab some bananas on your way over."

He laughed. "I'll do that. Thank you."

In a few minutes, they were at Jodi's door. She sensed Jim was in no hurry for the evening to end. The thought that they were both single flashed through Jodi's mind, making her uneasy in a not unpleasant way.

"Can you find your way to Kel's?" she asked quickly.

"I have my flashlight and the island is too small for me to get lost." He extended his hand. "I really enjoyed the evening, Jodi. Thank you for dinner and for the good company."

She placed her hand in his. "I enjoyed it, too, Jim. See you bright and early." She turned away abruptly, as if unwilling to trust herself.

Jim moved through the palms, along the same path Jodi had taken him on earlier, his flashlight beam dancing on the ground in front of him. He could hear the ocean and the rustling of the palm fronds above him. He paused and glanced back toward Jodi's hut. Spotting the flicker of her kerosene lantern through the trees, he was vaguely discomfited by stirrings he hadn't experienced for years.

Life's full of surprises, he thought.

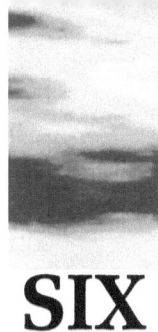

SIX

Jodi had water boiling when Jim arrived, bananas in one hand, a towel and bottle of water in the other. He wore a tee shirt and swimming trunks. They were soon sitting on the beach, breakfasting on bananas and instant coffee in the murky grey light of early dawn. A pink glow was just visible on the horizon.

"Sleep well?" Jodi asked.

"Very well, thanks. It rained pretty heavily during the night."

"It looks like we'll have a clear morning. Did you bring sunscreen?"

"I should have picked some up in Honolulu but it slipped my mind."

"I have a tube we can share."

Jim noticed a pair of terns skimming the ocean surface. "It's so peaceful here. This must be the way all these islands were at one time."

"That was a long time ago. Ever since Captain Marshall stopped here in 1788, it's been downhill. First came the whalers, then the missionaries. After that the islands were colonized by the Germans, then by the Japanese, and finally by the Americans. Paradise lost."

He shook his head. "And there are plenty of people who call that progress. No turning back the clock, I'm afraid. Speaking of which, will Mero be waiting for us?"

Jodi laughed. "Promptness isn't a Marshallese trait. When he said sunrise, he meant any time between the first faint glow and nine o'clock. The most difficult thing when dealing with the Marshallese is to pin them down. They hate to refuse a request, so even when they say yes to something, they don't always go through with it. But Mero is reliable."

"Is he the only one with an outboard?"

"Yes. The other fishermen only have canoes and they mostly stay within the lagoon."

"I hope my diving gear will fit in the boat."

"We might as well head over and find out. Let me just get my stuff together."

Mero was tinkering with his outboard engine as Jim and Jodi approached. His sons stood on either side of him, watching intently as Mero made adjustments. He returned Jodi's greeting of "Yokwe" and smiled as he spoke.

"He says he'll be ready to go in a few minutes. We might as well get your diving gear."

They piled everything on the dock and Mero indicated for Jim to place his gear at the bow end.

"There'll barely be enough room for us," said Jim, good-naturedly.

"We can rest the tank between us on the seat," Jodi suggested.

Mero's boys handed him two fishing rods once he was seated in the stern. He then shook his head at what they asked him and Jodi laughed.

"They wanted to know if he could squeeze them into the boat."

"So even though we've rented the boat, he doesn't want to miss a morning's fishing," said Jim.

"On this island," replied Jodi, "fish is more valuable than money. After you see what Kel has on his shelves, you'll understand."

Mero pulled the outboard out of the water as his two boys pushed the boat away from shore, then dropped it back in postion. Mero's wife watched from the doorway of the hut holding the baby in her arms.

The engine caught on the first pull and they moved smoothly across the lagoon. Mero was intent on steering the craft as Jodi and Jim sat facing him. The rising sun was warm on their shoulders. Jodi offered the sunblock to Jim.

"Want me to do your back?" Jim asked.

"Sure, then I'll do yours."

As his hand moved over Jodi's back, he realized how long it had been since he had stroked a woman's skin. He envisioned Aiko in bed with him and tried to remember what she felt like.

"My turn," Jodi said, interrupting his thoughts.

Jim unconsciously flinched as Jodi touched him, responding to the sensuous feelings aroused by Aiko's memory. Jodi's hand paused, then quickly finished.

"Thanks," he said, as Jodi twisted the top on the tube. Their eyes met and Jodi smiled.

"Thank you," she said, quietly.

As Mero headed through the opening in the reef, they felt the surge of the ocean current. Spray from surf breaking off to their right misted their backs. Jodi turned and looked at the horizon.

"Nice and calm this morning. No whitecaps and not much wind."

A half hour later Mero turned off the engine and the boat glided to a halt, gently bobbing on the water. As Mero spoke, Jodi translated. "He says this is the spot where he first sighted the dolphins. Then, as he came nearer, they moved off. He says he should have known this behavior was a bad omen. It was here he hit something and saw blood in the water. The arm was caught in the propeller and the head was over there. He didn't see any other parts."

"There aren't any dolphins today," Jim observed. "I don't know if that's a good or a bad sign. I might as well take a look and see if there's anything down there. You done any diving?"

"Only snorkeling. I'm afraid I won't be of much help."

"Well, you can give me a hand with my gear."

Jodi held the unit while Jim thrust his arms through the shoulder straps. He bent forward balancing the tank on his back as he tightened the straps. After adjusting the weight belt, Jim smeared saliva on the inside of his mask, then rinsed it in the ocean. He slipped the mask on, and then his fins.

"No need for a wet suit?" Jodi asked.

"The water is warm out here and I won't be down that long. Mind shifting your weight to that side?"

Mero watched quietly as Jodi leaned starboard. Jim eased down on the port edge. Fitting the regulator to his mouth, he gave a thumbs up and backrolled over. The boat tilted sharply, then righted as Newell disappeared.

For several moments, Jodi stared at the spot where he had entered, then took a deep breath as she glanced around her. She could make out the palms of Illetto in the distance beyond the reef. Off the starboard side, in a southeasterly direction, she noticed a small island barely visible. Jodi guessed it was at least five miles away.

"What island is that, Mero?" she asked, pointing.

He followed the direction of her finger, then looked away without answering.

Jodi turned to him. "Mero?"

"That is the island of evil."

"Is that its name?"

"That is what my people call it."

"Does anyone live there?"

"It's best you ask Mister Monna."

Puzzled, Jodi decided to drop the subject. But she certainly would ask Mister Monna about it. The island was not visible from the beach. If she hadn't come out today, she would never have known it was there. Jodi had always thought Illetto was an isolated island with Ailinginae atoll, at least fifteen miles to the east, its nearest neighbor.

Mero slowly baited his hooks with squid and cast both lines out to the east, away from where Jim was exploring. He concentrated on his fishing, oblivious to the diver beneath the surface. But Jodi moved nervously from side to side in the boat. She glanced at her watch, uneasily watching the minutes pass. After thirty-five minutes she was almost frantic. She was about to say something to Mero when Jim suddenly surfaced off the port side. He swam over and grasped the side. Removing mask and mouthpiece, he shook his head.

"Nice fish but not much else. I'm coming up."

Mero, with fish hooked on both lines, ignored the rocking of the boat as Jim hoisted himself aboard. Jodi kept her weight on the starboard side until he was on, then helped remove his gear.

"I was getting a little worried," she said.

He smiled at her as he pulled off his fins. "You don't have to be. I know what I'm doing." He motioned toward Mero, now reeling quickly on one rod while watching the other. "Besides, if I got in trouble I'd pull on one of his lines and he'd bring me in."

Mero quickly tossed the fish, two red snappers each weighing about five pounds, into the boat. Happy with this fishing spot, he baited the hooks again and cast out the lines.

"I think he's forgotten why we're here," said Jim. He tipped his head back and drank deeply from his water bottle, then turned to Jodi.

"You know, I don't think it was a coincidence that the dolphins swam away from him. He's right about it being unusual. In fact, it's almost unheard of. I've been on Scripps vessels where we had dolphins swimming with us for hundreds of miles, just having a great old time leaping and diving. There had to be a reason why they shied away and I think I know what it was."

His grey eyes were focused on Jodi but he was preoccupied with his own thoughts.

She waited eagerly. "I think they were protecting something. Perhaps that creature Mero hit. And others like it. Jodi, ask if our fisherman will do some cruising. Tell him we're looking for dolphins."

"Jolok bod," Jodi said, pointing in the distance.

Mero, disappointed at having to leave a good fishing area, shrugged and reeled in his lines. But he quickly started the engine and steered the boat northwest. Jodi told Jim about the island and Mero's reaction to her questions.

"That's something we'll have to look into when we get back," he replied.

For the next two hours they moved ahead but there were no dolphins. Illetto receded further and further in the distance.

"I think we'll have to call it a day," Jim said finally. "You've got your clinic this afternoon. Let's ask him to head in."

Relieved, Mero swung the boat around and opened the throttle.

"He's anxious to get back. Ask him if he'll take us out tomorrow."

"He says that would be fine, provided he can do some fishing."

Jim was deep in thought during the trip back. They were soon at the beach and helped Mero drag the boat up. Jim then unloaded his gear and disassembled and cleaned the regulator before storing the equipment back in the duffel bag.

"You seem preoccupied," said Jodi, watching him carefully.

"I'm a little worried, to be honest. I think the dolphins are the key to our search. But that's a big ocean out there. If they remain elusive, then how long do we keep searching? And if we do spot dolphins, what if it's not the same group Mero saw?"

"You're convinced it's one particular group?"

"I'm assuming that because of their behavior. And let's face it. Even though it's a guess, we have so little to go on we might as well head in that direction and see where it leads us."

"I wonder if that other island is tied into this somehow."

"How can we find out?"

"Mero said I should talk to Mister Monna. He's the headman in Illetto. I have to be in the clinic this afternoon, but if you'd like we can meet at about five at my house and go see him together."

"Great. Can we do dinner again?"

"I've got some canned goods. You might check to see what Kel has on his shelves and if anything strikes your fancy, bring it along."

"Will do. And I'll explore the island while you work. See you at five."

"Walk slowly," Jodi called as he headed for the path. "Otherwise you'll be done in ten minutes."

He laughed and waved. Jodi's thoughts were rushing as she watched him disappear. That theory about the dolphins was such a wild guess. But he was right about one thing. They had very little to go on. And even if this plan led to a dead end, she enjoyed his company. Jodi smiled to herself at the incongruity of meeting a man she liked on a postage stamp-size island in the middle of the Pacific Ocean.

Her afternoon was uneventful until four when a teen-aged boy suddenly appeared in the doorway, tears glistening on his brown face. "Doctor Jodi," he cried, "I'm in such pain."

The Marshallese were usually stoical and it was very unusual to see a young man cry.

"Where?" she asked.

He pointed to his leg. A portion of the tentacle of a box-jellyfish was stuck to the skin. Jodi hurried to her supply shelf for a bottle of vinegar.

"Quickly," she said, "lie down on the table."

Jodi poured half the contents over the area, paralyzing the tentacle nematocysts to stop the venom discharge. She then took a forceps and carefully peeled off the tentacle, dropping it into a tin can. Later she would burn it. A dark stripe with some blistering had appeared on the boy's skin, but his pain was easing.

"Where were you when this happened?" she asked.

"On the east side near the rocks. I was wading through a shallow pool when I got stung."

"I want you to rest on the table for a while until I'm sure you're okay."

The Marshallese called the box-jellyfish a sea wasp. It was the most venomous creature in the sea. Each one carried enough poison to kill three adults. It was something Jodi was always on the lookout for when she went swimming. While in Ebeye, she had been on the beach when a man came out of the water with several long tentacles hanging from his body. He collapsed and died before anyone could help. An antivenin was available but there was none in the islands.

The boy, embarrassed now by his tears, wiped at them with the back of his hand.

"The pain is less now," he said.

"You were lucky. You've got to watch out for these sea wasps before stepping in the water. They're more dangerous than sharks."

The boy slowly sat up. "I'll go now. Thank you."

"That will hurt for a while," Jodi said. "Take these two tablets now for the pain." She handed him a glass of water. "And here's two more. You can take them in about four hours if it's still hurting."

Jodi then closed up the clinic and headed for home. Jim was just approaching from the other direction, a box under his arm.

"My goodness, what did you bring?" Jodi asked, smiling.

"All sorts of goodies." He pulled out three cans of tuna, two cans of soup, a box of biscuits and some canned vegetables. "Half of this stuff comes from Japan."

"I know," said Jodi. "Even the tuna. The Japanese boats catch tons of it here, can it, then sell it back to the Marshallese at inflated prices. You really didn't have to bring so much. I have enough in the house."

"Well, you won't have enough for long if I keep cleaning you out. You have to let me contribute my share. Shall we go to see the headman before we start dinner?"

"What did you do this afternoon?" Jodi asked, as they walked.

"Well, I followed your advice and walked slowly but I still covered the entire island in a half-hour. Then I did some reading, went for a swim and bought the groceries. Kel and I chatted as best we could with his limited English. I asked him about that little island. I don't know if he couldn't understand or simply didn't want to talk about it. What about you? Any exciting cases?"

"A box-jellyfish sting."

"That's a nasty creature. How's your patient?"

"Fine. He had only a small piece attached."

"Lucky. When it comes to venom, the box-jellyfish puts the Portuguese Man of War to shame. Australia has a real problem with them."

Mister Monna, carrying a coconut in his hands, was just entering his house as they approached. Jodi called to him and he turned. His black, wrinkled face broke into a smile when he recognized her. Jodi shook hands with the old man and introduced Jim.

"Come in out of the sun," he said. "Shall I get some coconuts for you?"

"No, thank you, Mister Monna. Do you have time to talk?"

The old man made a clucking sound. "Do I have time? I have nothing but time." He arranged some mats on the floor of the hut and the three sat facing one another.

"Will Doctor Jim be working on Illetto, too?"

"No," said Jodi. "He's just visiting. We were out on Mero Attri's boat today, beyond the reef, and we noticed a small island to the southeast. I'd never seen it before. I asked Mero about it, but he told me I should talk to you."

Mister Monna sighed. "It is not something I like to talk about."

"Mero called it the island of evil."

The old man nodded. "It has another name, but for many years now that is what it has been called."

"Please tell us why."

Jim sat quietly, not understanding a word of the conversation but searching their faces intently for clues. He could tell Monna was reluctant to talk.

"It was the year of the bomb test, the one you call Bravo. On that day, as you know, there was a group of us here gathering coconuts and eggs. Six of the women with us were pregnant." His aged, rheumy eyes stared vacantly at the wall, as if he were visualizing that time in the past. "The first three had their babies in Ailinginae. All were born healthy, although as the years passed they developed that problem here." He pointed to his neck and Jodi knew he meant they had thyroid nodules.

"When we returned to Illetto, many months later, the other three had still not had their babies. One of them went into labor the day we arrived here to gather coconuts."

He paused and looked directly at Jodi. "She had a baby that was . . . "
He groped for words. "It was not a human baby," he said finally, his
voice so soft Jodi wasn't sure she had heard correctly.

"I don't understand," she said.

"It was a boychild, that we could see. But it had the head of a
fish."

Jodi translated for Jim, his eyes fixed on the old man.

"Ask him to describe the head."

Monna was silent for several seconds, as if trying to recall
something. "The eyes were the eyes of a baby. But instead of a nose it
had one round opening. The mouth had no lips, just a long slit. And on
the sides of the head were gills, like on a fish."

"Was the baby alive?" Jodi asked.

"It appeared to be alive. The mother, when she saw it, began to
scream. We decided that it would be best to put the creature to death."

"Did you . . . ?"

"On the northwest end of the island there is an inlet where the
ocean flows into the lagoon. If you were out with Mero, you know
where I mean. A little beyond that, further to the west, there is a
smaller opening in the reef. At certain times, many sharks come in
there. You can often see their fins. We call that place the shark pit. We
took the baby out there in one of our canoes and threw it into the
water."

Jodi's voice trembled as she translated.

"The other two women, who were also near their time, knew what
had happened. They were too frightened to return to Ailinginae. If
something was wrong with their babies, they did not want their
families to see. So we waited here for them to go into labor. In less
than two weeks, they gave birth."

"And their babies?"

"Both girls, but they, too, had fish heads."

Jodi turned to Jim. She swallowed hard, trying to find her voice.
"My God, Jim. They all had the same abnormality."

"Did you throw those babies into the sea also?" she asked quietly.

The old man nodded. "Into the shark pit."

"Jodi," interrupted Jim, "ask if the babies' heads were more like
dolphin heads than fish heads."

Monna's expression was thoughtful. "Yes," he replied, "except for the gills."

"How terrible for the mothers," said Jodi. "What happened to them?"

"We did not want this evil to happen again so they were sent to another island, the one you saw. No man was allowed to go to there. Not even our young women would visit them. They were afraid that the curse would be placed upon them and that they would have babies with fish heads. Only their mothers or old women would go to that island."

"But, Mister Monna, weren't you aware that the radiation from the bomb could have caused the children to be like that?"

"Afterward, we thought about that. I did not tell you this the last time we spoke, but on the day of two suns those of us who were on Illetto gathering coconuts and eggs were covered with the yellow powder that came from the sky. Later, when we were back on Ailinginae, we heard that the people from Rongelap and Utrik had been taken from their islands because of this powder. But, Doctor Jodi, there were other women who were pregnant when they were on Illetto that day. They had children without fish heads. That is why we believed that the evil eye had only been put on the women who bore fish heads."

After Jodi translated, Jim commented wryly, "I don't suppose it would do much good to try to explain to him about fetal age at the time of any radiation exposure."

"Mister Monna," said Jodi, "all this happened more than forty years ago. Are those women still alone on that island?"

"They are all dead now. Our people finally decided to let them live among us again. We sent Anjain to speak to them, but they refused to come back. 'It has been too long,' they said. 'This island is now our home.' That is where they wished to die—and that is where they died. All of them."

"How sad," said Jodi. "Who is Anjain?"

"She is a woman of my age who was with us on Illetto when the women had their children. She helped them at the births and then threw the fish heads to the sharks."

"She still lives here?"

"Yes. If you wish to see her, I will tell her."

"We would like to talk to her," said Jodi.

As Jodi and Jim got up to leave, the old man stood and touched her arm. "Doctor Jodi, this bad thing happened long ago. It is something my people would like to forget. Nothing that terrible has befallen us since. Please do not talk to others about this."

"I . . . I don't know if I can make that promise, Mister Monna. We'll talk more about this after we see . . . " She paused.

"Anjain," offered Mister Monna.

"Yes."

"I will send her to you this evening."

Jodi and Jim returned to Jodi's hut in silence. The last pink traces of sunset were just tinging the sky to the west while above them dusk was rapidly settling in. They could already see the moon. Neither of them was hungry so they walked along the beach.

"Let's sit here," Jodi said.

They watched as crabs scurried along the water's edge, pausing only to hold fast when the surf covered them.

Jodi lowered her head, one hand over her eyes.

"Are you all right?" asked Jim.

Tears welled in her eyes as she looked over at him. "I keep thinking of those poor women, sent into exile for something they had no control over. It makes me so angry. Not at the Marshallese. They were all victims and didn't know any better. But at our own people who did this."

Tears rolled down her cheeks. Instinctively, Jim started to put his arms around her, but thought better of it.

"I'm sorry," Jodi said hoarsely, not noticing. "It all seems so tragic."

Just then there was a sound behind them and they turned to see an elderly woman moving slowly toward them across the sand. "Yokwe," she said, her voice almost a croak. She squatted beside them.

"Anjain?" asked Jodi, brushing tears away.

The mass of wrinkles on the woman's face rearranged themselves into a smile.

Jodi, trying to regain her composure, cleared her throat. "Anjain, can you tell us anything about the babies that were born here after the day of two suns, the ones that were not normal."

The smile slowly disappeared. "Those babies were children of evil."

"This doctor and I would like to know exactly how they looked."

"Their heads had gills like fish. Their eyes were human, but they had no nose, only an opening that looked like the hole on a dolphin's head. Their mouths had no lips and no tongue."

"And their bodies?"

"From the chest down they were normal children. One was a male child and two were female."

"Did they have webbed fingers?"

The old woman shook her head.

"And they were all alive when they were born?"

"Yes."

"Were they still alive when you took them to the shark pit?"

The woman's eyes narrowed.

"Mister Monna told us, Anjain. It's all right."

"They were alive when I threw them into the water."

"Jodi," interrupted Jim, "ask her what happened after they were in the water. Did they try to swim? Did she see any sharks? Were there any dolphins in the area?"

"She says she turned her back immediately after throwing them in. She can't tell us any more."

Jodi thanked her for coming and the old woman shuffled up the beach mumbling to herself as she disappeared among the coconut palms.

"That didn't add much, did it?"

"No, I guess not," Jim replied. "But it confirms everything Monna told us, and . . . "

"And?"

"Why don't we get some dinner going. That'll give me a chance to ponder it a bit more."

"If you'll play boy scout again and make the fire, I'll run up to the house and get everything together."

Jodi soon returned with the box Jim had brought. Piled on top were dishes, a pot, and a kettle. "Ready for a can opener special?" she asked.

Jim, waving a palm leaf to encourage the fire, laughed. "As long as I don't have to eat any more bananas today."

70

"Have you finished pondering?" Jodi asked as they had their soup.

"This is all guesswork, you understand," said Jim, putting his dish in his lap. "What do we know so far? We know three abnormal babies were thrown into the ocean. They all were born with the same abnormality, but I don't think the gills were functional. Just visceral arch remnants. Remember, Anjain said the babies were alive when she took them out to the shark pit. Considering the time that had elapsed from the moment of birth until the canoe got them out on the water, we just have to assume they had mammalian respiratory systems. Those fetuses must have received an intense dose of radiation, not enough to kill them but enough to affect their cranial development. Judging by the fact that they were all born about the same time, they must have been at the same stage of development when the fallout covered Illetto.

"Knowing all this, we have to assume they survived after they were thrown into the water. In spite of the fact that the Marshallese call the area the shark pit, that doesn't mean that sharks are always there. There was a fad in the States not so long ago, you may remember, when some parents tried to teach their infants to swim. I was intrigued when I watched the films of those little babies automatically making swimming motions and in some cases, actually swimming. Now, obviously, human infants couldn't survive for long in an aquatic environment. Those babies needed their parents to attend to them.

"That's where I believe the dolphins come in. Dolphins are true mammals, they're warm-blooded, they have a four-chambered heart, they bear live young, they nurse them, and—they have to teach their young to survive. When a dolphin calf is born, it has no air in its lungs. If it's not assisted by the mother or other dolphins, it will sink and suffocate. The adults nudge it up to the water's surface for air. A dolphin calf can only remain submerged for about thirty seconds."

Noticing Jodi's open mouth, he laughed. "You think I'm crazy, right?"

"No, I'm fascinated. Go on."

"Well, what if dolphins happened to be there when the babies were tossed into the water? It's known that dolphins will come to the aid of a dolphin that's disabled. They buoy it up so it can breathe, or they nudge it into shallower water. I've even heard of dolphins coming to the rescue of swimmers who were drowning. Isn't it possible that the dolphins would have kept the babies afloat, assisting them to the surface when necessary, and also nursing them? Remember, the bodies of these infants were human in form, but in other respects they resembled dolphins.

"I know all this smacks of science fiction, but if what I've said is possible, and the babies survived to become part of a dolphin school, protected by the adults, then as time passed they would have matured. Procreation would have been possible. There were two females and one male. Remember, Anjain said she didn't see any webbing of the fingers. But we know the creature Mero killed had webbed fingers and that had to have come from somewhere.

"Forty-four years have passed since Bravo. That's enough time for three generations. And with each succeeding generation, isn't it likely that changes would occur to help them adapt? Like webbed fingers to make them more efficient swimmers? The ancestors of dolphins were land mammals. When they returned to the sea, they underwent gradual changes."

"If what you say is true, Jim, there could be dozens of these creatures by now."

"That's right. And wouldn't that also explain the behavior of the dolphins Mero saw? Dolphins are intelligent creatures. They like to be petted and stroked and, in fact, will seek out human company. But this school of dolphins didn't. They must know these half-dolphin, half-human creatures are vulnerable.

"I've told you that I've watched dolphins playing around a ship for hours at a time, swimming hundreds of miles without tiring. I can't imagine these half-dolphin creatures have evolved to that point. The dolphins must be protecting them against anything that's threatening . . . "

"It's a compelling argument."

He gave a short laugh. "You're right, Jodi, but . . . All we have to do is prove it."

"I was thinking. Even if everything you've said is true, then what? What will happen when word gets out? I just wish none of this had ever happened."

"Look, even if Mero hadn't hit that thing it was probably inevitable that they'd be discovered. One could have been trapped in a fish net or spotted by a diver."

"I guess you're right," she said, opening two cans of tuna and passing one to Jim. "It's not much of a dinner, I'm afraid."

"I'd rather be sitting on this beach with you and eating tuna than sitting in the best restaurant in La Jolla."

Jodi felt her heart jump. She threw him a quick glance and asked playfully: "Is that because you like tuna so much?"

They just looked at one another for a few moments. Jim started to speak, then looked down and picked at his food. They ate in silence, not wanting to disturb this new emotion between them.

"Well, I guess we'll have to wait and see what tomorrow brings," Jodi said as they were gathering things up. "I really don't know if I want Mero to find those dolphins."

Jim, a thoughtful expression on his face, quietly followed Jodi as they headed to her hut.

"I'll light the lantern," she said as they entered.

He gently touched her arm. "Jodi, I want you to know I share some of your fears. If I am right, I don't know what will happen, how people—governments—will respond. I've been so focused on just finding these creatures, that I've tried not to give that too much thought. But I'm not sorry this happened. If it hadn't . . . "

He winced as Aiko's face flashed through his thoughts. "I'd better say goodnight. See you in the morning. Thanks for dinner."

He turned and quickly disappeared into the darkness, not bothering to use his flashlight. Jodi stared after him into the night and rubbed her arm where Jim had touched her.

SEVEN

Light rain was falling as Mero Attri steered his boat through the breach in the coral reef. Jodi and Jim cradled the air tank between them on the seat.

Jim looked apprehensively at the sky. "If the rain gets any heavier, I don't know if we should stay out. There's not much visibility."

"I'm sure Mero will tell us if he thinks we should head back."

They hadn't talked much this morning. Jodi, still troubled by their abrupt parting the evening before, tried to put her mind at ease. She liked Jim Newell and enjoyed being with him but a serious relationship was the furthest thing from her mind. She suspected that Jim had warm feelings toward her. Those sentiments had almost found expression after he touched her arm. This is a man to be wary of, she thought to herself. It seemed he had never come to terms with his wife's death and she had no intention of playing therapist. If there was one thing she did not need, it was another failed relationship.

Several times Jim started to speak, then checked himself. Jodi stared off in the distance but her real gaze was inward.

With Mero facing them, their reserve only increased. They seemed like two strangers forced to share a seat on a boat destined for nowhere.

As much as he hoped to find the dolphins, Jim found himself wishing the rain would set in so they could return to shore. More than anything he felt the need to overcome the awkwardness that lay between them.

Jim watched Mero's face carefully. The fisherman stared impassively ahead of him, but suddenly moved his head to the side and squinted. He quickly cut their speed and Jodi and Jim turned in their seats to follow Mero's gaze. A dark cloud in the distance seemed to merge with the sea but at its base they could make out some movement on the water's surface.

As they approached, dolphins were jumping out of the water, their bodies a flash of grey and white. Others stood almost erect on their tail flippers, their white undersides facing the boat.

"You see," Mero said to Jodi, an undercurrent of fear in his voice. "Their behavior is as I said. They will not come to us. If I get any closer, they might swim away."

She translated for Jim, who was getting his gear together.

"Tell him I'll go in here and try to approach them under the water."

"Jim, I don't like your diving alone. What happened to the buddy system I've heard about among scuba divers? If anything happens to you down there, Mero and I wouldn't be able to help."

"I'm not going to do anything rash so don't worry. Besides, there's less chance of spooking the dolphins with just one of us. Here, help me get this on."

The dolphins kept their distance but showed no sign of swimming away. Mero cut his engine. The rain had now stopped and the winds had blown the clouds south.

"They're so beautiful," said Jodi, watching the dolphins. The details of their bodies were now visible against the clearing sky behind them.

Jim sat on the boat's edge and his eyes met Jodi's as she shifted her weight to the other side of the boat. They both felt the tension between them melt away.

"Be careful," she said as Jim rolled off the boat.

As Jodi concentrated on the ocean between the boat and the school of dolphins, Mero Attri baited his hooks. He had promised to bring enough fish for everyone in his family. The dolphins' behavior might be strange but he hoped they would bring him luck. In the past that had always been the case. School of dolphins, school of fish, Mero murmured to himself, trying not to think of the day of his accident.

Jim Newell was thinking of Jodi as he checked the lubber line on his wrist compass. Never once in the years since Aiko's death had he thought about another woman. His energies had been too focused on work and his two daughters. And although he knew little about Jodi except that she wasn't married, he sensed something had happened in the past to hurt her and that she, too, had not been close with anyone for a long time.

When he opened his eyes this morning, it was with the previous night's parting in his thoughts. He knew what words were left unsaid, that if Mero Attri had not had his collision with the sea creature, he and Jodi would never have met. But by admitting to himself that he was glad fate had arranged their meeting, he felt he had betrayed the memory of Aiko. In his deepest being he knew he had found someone special, someone he would like to know better. But for that to happen he had to accept the fact that Aiko was gone. It was something he had not permitted himself to do. He realized now that he had never grieved properly, that he had only immersed himself in work, always imagining that was what Aiko would have wanted him to do.

He forced his attention back to the matter at hand. Checking his depth gauge, he noted that he was twenty feet below the surface. That was adequate for his approach. Visibility was good, probably one hundred feet, and the water was warm. He had no idea how deep the ocean was at this point but the bottom was nowhere in sight. The tropical fish swimming past were brilliantly colored, their shimmering blues and yellows making a kaleidoscope of the water. Under different circumstances, he would have tried to identify them. But there were only two things to concentrate on now: dolphins and sharks.

Jodi was right about his diving alone. No one knew that better than Jim. During his first expedition with Scripps Institute, he and another diver, Peter Landis, had explored the Coral Sea Basin waters halfway between the Solomon Islands and the east coast of Australia. They were down about forty feet with no more than ten feet separating them when Jim had felt something brush his legs. Only seconds later, Peter was fighting off a tiger shark. Knife in hand, Jim had instantly gone to his assistance. During the struggle, he had felt a searing pain in his right hip but he was able to plunge his knife into the shark's eye.

The two men surfaced rapidly, both seriously wounded. By the time the boat picked them up Peter was unconscious, a major artery in his arm severed. Jim was also in danger of passing out from blood loss. He had extensive muscle damage to his right hip. It had left him with a large jagged scar from the debridement and repair done at the hospital in Brisbane. Fortunately, his swimsuit always covered the area.

That incident had increased his alertness, but a diver never knows what lurks in the waters. Shark attacks are rare, he told himself. But as with lightning storms, it can just be a case of being in the wrong place at the wrong time.

In the distance, he spotted several dark shapes headed for the surface. They were at least one hundred feet away. He swam ten feet closer, then held his position.

At least twenty dolphins, each eight or ten feet long, were cavorting in the water. If they were aware of his presence, there was no sign of alarm. There was nothing haphazard about their swimming; they seemed to maintain a circle in the water even as they streaked for the surface, then dived again.

Suddenly he saw them.

They were inside that circle, too far away to make out details. At first he thought they were dolphins but their appendages were not fins. They were arms and legs. Slowly, Jim approached. He counted at least four. They swam gracefully but it was like watching children trying to compete with the world's finest Olympic divers.

Then, as Jim closed to about sixty feet away, the dolphins closed ranks. In tight formation, they swam away. He could no longer see the four creatures. To pursue them, he knew, would be futile. He checked his compass and headed back. Emerging behind the boat's stern he caught a glimpse of Jodi scanning the water. She waved as she spotted him.

He quickly climbed aboard and took off his gear. Excited, he grabbed her hands.

"I saw them."

"So did I," she replied, squeezing his hands. "There must have been at least twenty. They were leaping out of the water and then all of a sudden they took off in that direction." She pointed to the northeast. "Look, they're getting further and further away."

"Jodi, I'm not talking about the dolphins."

She stared at him, then turned as Mero spoke.

"He wants to know if you plan to keep looking for dolphins."

"Not today. But I'd like to come back tomorrow."

"He's only caught one fish," Jodi said, exasperated by Mero's interruptions. "Do you mind if he fishes a little longer before we head back?"

"That's fine," replied Jim, noticing the lone snapper flopping on the deck near Mero Attri's feet. Quickly gathering his thoughts, he turned back to Jodi.

"There were at least four of them. Four of the creatures like Mero hit. The dolphins were swimming in a circle protecting them."

"My God! Are you sure?"

"Absolutely. I would have taken photos but I couldn't get close enough. But I saw them, Jodi. They had human bodies—two arms and two legs."

"Can we follow them?"

He shook his head. "No. Maybe the next time they see me they'll let me get closer. If we go looking for them now they might think we're pursuing them. At least we know they're here. I'm sure they'll be back. We can try again tomorrow."

Mero had pulled in two more fish. Noting Jim and Jodi's excitement, he baited his hooks.

"Ask him about tomorrow."

Mero nodded. The Americans were bringing him luck with his fishing and paying him besides.

"Should we tell him, Jim?"

"No, that would only alarm him. Let him think I've been investigating the dolphins."

Mero caught seven more fish during the next hour, three of them small tuna. He was about to bait his hooks again when Jodi said she had to get to the clinic.

Without a word, and eager to show his family what a good day it had been, he turned the boat toward shore.

"There's a happy man," said Jim.

At the dock Mero handed a snapper to Jodi.

"Looks like we have fish for dinner again," she said.

"Kommool tata, Mero."

Jim stored his diving gear and then walked Jodi to the clinic. His underwater adventure played over and over in his mind. Jodi, too, could think of nothing else. If just anyone had told her four half-human creatures were swimming with a school of dolphins, she would have been incredulous. But Jim Newell was not someone with a runaway imagination.

No one was waiting as they approached the clinic. They entered and awkwardly faced each other, neither knowing what to say.

Fumbling for words, Jim tried to break the silence. "Jodi, last night I . . . uh . . . " Hearing children's voices, he paused. "I'll see you for dinner," he said, stepping aside as two children and their mother entered.

"You'd better put this fish in water," she said, smiling and handing him the red snapper.

Jim wandered about the island, often retracing his steps without being aware of it. It was only when he noticed the sun disappearing over the horizon that he realized the time. It was almost six when he appeared at Jodi's, the fish in a bucket suspended from his arm and a coconut in each hand.

"This one is a merlot," he said, indicating the one on the right, "and the other is a sauvignon blanc. We should probably start with the white." His humor, he knew, was forced and now that he was again alone with Jodi, he was suddenly shy.

"You had a radio call from Bikini a half hour ago," she said, a half-serious look on her face.

"Oh?" He felt a sudden chill, his first thought being concern for his daughters.

"Doctor Chambers wants to know if you have any news."

Jim, suddenly angry, let out an explosive "damn!"

"She herself questioned how confidential these radio calls are and now she wants me to tell her if I have any news? Sometimes I wonder."

"Shall I take that as a negative for sending an answer?"

"Definitely a negative. Let's wait and see what happens tomorrow."

During dinner Jodi stared distractedly at the ocean. The breeze coming off the water ruffled her blond hair.

"What are you thinking?" Jim asked quietly.

"I was wondering what will come of all this."

"The sea creatures?"

"Them. And other things."

"I've been thinking about that all day," Jim said, placing his fork on his dish. A few strands of hair had blown across Jodi's face and he resisted the urge to touch them.

"And?"

"Where should I begin? With the creatures or with other things?"

"Wherever you wish."

"I was abrupt last night and I'd like to explain . . . "

"You don't owe me any explanations."

"Please. This isn't easy for me to talk about. Since my wife's death, I've thought only of my work and the raising of my two daughters. Now, with both girls in college, I know it's time to give some thought to the rest of my own life. I think you know how much I like you." He smiled and gave an embarrassed laugh. "Well, that's not the right word. I'm really fond of you, Jodi. I'd like us to get to know one another better. I've really had a hard time dealing with Aiko's death, but it is time. If you'd be patient with . . . "

"Jim, look, I like you, too, but you have to go back to California and I have another year in the Marshalls."

"We can work all that out."

Jodi shook her head, a skeptical smile on her lips. "It's just not practical. You've only known me for a few days. You know nothing about me."

"I know what I feel, Jodi."

"I can be very difficult. I've had two serious relationships and both went sour because I can't be what men want me to be. Are you sure you want a relationship with an independent woman?"

"Just because my wife was Japanese doesn't mean she was submissive. Aiko was far too intelligent for that."

"I wasn't referring to that. I meant that men in general like to call the shots and have their women go along with them. I don't think I can do that, no matter what I feel."

"Maybe that's part of the attraction, Jodi."

"But there are so many obstacles. All I've known is third-world medicine. It's what I love. You have a career in the States. You're known and respected. I wouldn't consider doing private practice at this point. Even academic medicine doesn't interest me. I like what I'm doing, Jim."

"Do you think I'd try to prevent you?"

"I don't think relationships can grow when they involve long periods of separation."

"We can both do the kind of medicine we want—and in the same place."

"But then I'd feel guilty about making you give up something."

"What if that's my choice?"

"It's foolish to talk about this. I can't get out of my contract with the Public Health Service."

"Hawaii is halfway between California and Kwaj. We can meet there until your year is up."

They looked into each other's eyes and neither spoke for several moments.

"You're serious about this."

"All I'm asking is for us to give it a chance, to see where it goes."

"What about your daughters? Wouldn't you miss them? And how would they feel about another woman?"

He laughed. "They'd be ecstatic. They've been dropping not so subtle hints for quite a while. 'It's really not good for you to be alone, dad.' 'You really should be going out more, dad.' And they're grown up, Jodi. They have their own lives."

They lay back on the sand and stared at the moon, obscured from time to time by drifting clouds. Lulled by the rustling of the palms in the breeze and the rhythmic breaking of surf on the beach, neither spoke.

"Will you let me think about it?" Jodi asked, breaking the silence.

"Of course."

"When do you have to go back to Kwaj?"

"That depends on the next sighting. I'd really like to get some photographs but I can't wait too long. Chambers was nervous about not reporting Mero's find. If I don't get back there, who knows what will happen? What we don't need is a leak to the newspapers."

"Will you head back to California after you talk to her?"

He turned to face her. "I'd like to come back here first."

"Good," said Jodi, sitting up. "But now, tell me about today."

"It's like a dream and hard to explain. I wish I could have gotten closer."

"Maybe tomorrow. At least we know these things are real. That gives us a lot to think about."

By the time they had cleaned their dishes, the fire had died down. The moon was now hidden behind the clouds as they walked toward Jodi's hut.

"It's been an exciting day," she said as they stood at her door.

"Yes, it has," Jim said, feeling awkward again. "I'd better let you get some sleep."

He placed his hands gently on Jodi's shoulders, barely touching her, then quickly kissed her cheek. "Good night, Jodi. See you bright and early."

EIGHT

"You liked the fish?" Mero asked as they loaded the boat.

"Delicious," replied Jodi, smiling.

"My family was happy. There was enough for everyone. Maybe today we can find more tuna."

Jim was busy adding a new tank to his diving gear in the boat. He then reached into his case and pulled out a spear gun.

"Are you expecting any trouble?" Jodi asked, alarmed.

"Not really. Just a precaution. I didn't mention it yesterday, but on my walk while you were in the clinic I spotted some fins near the reef. It's just better to have it handy."

"Jim, if there are sharks..."

"Jodi, there are always sharks in the ocean. Most of the time they're harmless. Come on, let's see if we can find those dolphins. I have a mask and snorkel for you."

Without asking, Mero automatically headed for their destination. The morning was sultry with barely a breeze and the glow of sunrise spread over the water's surface.

"You look worried," Jim said.

"It just makes me nervous when you're diving."

"Jodi, if the gun bothers you, I'll leave it in the boat."

"It's not the gun. I know you're an experienced diver, but if anything were to happen...."

"I don't take risks, Jodi. And I certainly wouldn't now." Forgetting the fisherman's presence, he looked purposefully into her eyes, his intense gaze unmistakable.

Mero smiled, saying something that made Jodi blush.

"What did he say?"

"He said he thinks you like me a lot," she replied hesitantly.

"Tell him he's right."

Jodi laughed. "I'll tell him no such thing."

"That's better. It's good to see you laughing. Those worrying frowns only give you wrinkles."

No dolphins were in sight when they reached their destination. Mero cruised slowly, searching the horizon. He pointed to several birds skimming the water far to the east.

"He wants to know if he should follow the birds."

Jim nodded. "Might as well. It looks like it will be hit or miss today. He's as anxious as we are to find the dolphins. Did you notice the third fishing rod?"

For almost an hour, Mero kept a northeasterly course. The birds had now disappeared and Illetto, many miles away, shimmered like a small jewel in the light of the risen sun. The smaller island that had been home for the unfortunate mothers of the abnormal children was clearly visible off the starboard bow.

"I wonder if their ghosts are watching us," said Jodi.

"I was thinking about them, too," replied Jim.

"We've lost the birds," said Mero. "Shall I head back west?"

Jim shrugged, scanning the horizon in every direction. "No matter what we do, it doesn't look promising. Tell him that's fine."

As the island known as evil receded into the distance, the fisherman suddenly pointed to the northwest. Jodi and Jim peered at the ocean's calm surface but could see nothing.

"There's something out there," Mero said, looking at Jodi.

Now they could see it. A small turbulence on the water like a lone whitecap.

"I think we've found them," said Mero, quietly.

They could soon make out the distinctive shapes of the dolphins performing their acrobatic leaps from the sea.

"Slow down. Let's get as close as we can," Jim said. "If it looks like we're making them nervous, we can pull back."

They closed to less than a hundred feet. The dolphins became agitated, their leaping and plunging roiling the ocean's surface.

"We'd better stop," said Jim.

He handed Jodi a mask and snorkel. "Don't get too far from the boat," he said, as she helped him with his tank.

"Don't worry about me. You be careful."

Mero, content to fish, was already baiting his hooks.

Jim rolled off the boat, then bobbed to the surface. "Jodi, you'd better hand me the gun. I'll feel more secure, especially with you in the water. Just in case we have unwanted visitors."

As Jodi entered the water, Jim disappeared beneath the surface. The water was so clear she could see him easily. With her mask on and snorkel in place, Jodi swam away from the boat. She could see the flashing dark shapes of the dolphins ahead of her. Jim was down about fifteen or twenty feet. He looked back at her and pointed.

It was then that Jodi saw them. Surrounded by the dolphins, they swam gracefully, rising to the surface for air, then diving. Jodi instantly noticed how they used their arms and legs like fins; their feet and hands were webbed. She was close enough to see that two of the creatures were males.

Jim kept his distance, watching the creatures intently, then slowly raised his camera. Suddenly, a dark shadow and a flurry of motion blocked him from Jodi's view. For a few seconds, she couldn't tell what was happening.

Jim and the dolphins had seen the tiger shark at the same time. Its twelve-foot body had streaked by just above him, the irregular stripes on its sides and fins unmistakable. The dolphins had reacted instantly, at least four ganging up on the shark. Jim watched as they took turns ramming its underside with their snouts. He had heard about this behavior but never seen it in person.

His sole concern now was that the shark might turn its attention to easier prey. Clipping his camera to his vest, he held his spear gun at the ready and ascended about ten feet, putting himself between the furor and Jodi. Jim knew that ordinarily tiger sharks would only go after sick or injured dolphins. Seeing the battle these dolphins put up, he could understand why.

Suddenly the square, blunted snout was headed directly at him. He raised the gun, quickly placing his finger on the release mechanism. But the shark twisted away and began warily circling the dolphins.

Jim knew from experience that although great whites received more publicity, the tiger shark was a more formidable enemy. More humans were killed by these ferocious creatures than by their larger cousins. When he had spotted those dorsal fins during his walk around the island, Jim had immediately suspected tiger sharks, known for feeding at coral reefs.

At that instant, the shark headed directly for the dolphins. Several dolphins again went on the attack, hurling themselves at its underside. Other dolphins took their place in the protective circle around the half-human creatures. Suddenly, as if dispirited by the fearless defence, the shark made an abrupt turn, passing within a meter of Jim, hovering in the water below Jodi.

Jim gripped his spear gun tightly as the sickle-shaped tail, its upper lobe almost half the length of the shark's body, swept by. Moments later the shark disappeared. With the immediate danger gone, the dolphins resumed their play, only this time, now more accustomed to the presence of the two humans, they swam closer. Jim could almost reach out and touch them. A few darted between him and Jodi, one breaching the surface next to them.

The four half-human creatures had also approached. Jim, taking photos, noticed that they surfaced more frequently than the dolphins, but spent only a few seconds at the surface. He quickly looked from one to the next. The silvery white sheen of the body gradually merged with the grey color of the prominent head. They were near enough now so he could make out the false gills of their visceral arches and the webbing between their fingers and toes. Their feet, human in shape, were long and wide. There was not much that could pass for body hair, although some was discernible in their pubic areas. The genitals of the two males were no different from that of a human male. But it was the eyes, the mournful brown eyes, that caught his attention. It was like looking at another human being.

Jim and Jodi, surrounded by dolphins, watched as the creatures swam up to them, arms extended. Jim reached out and touched the cold, alabaster skin of each outstretched hand that was offered. He glanced up to see Jodi tentatively stroking the back of one that glided past her. They seemed to enjoy this human contact as much as the dolphins, returning again and again.

Excited by their extraordinary contact with the fish heads, Jim had lost track of time. He checked his SPG, the gauge revealing very little air left in his tank. He signalled to Jodi that he was heading up.

"Jim, we've touched them!" Jodi shouted as Jim broke the surface next to her. Her eyes were wide with amazement.

They quickly swam to the stern as Mero was angrily reeling in his lines. "Too much commotion," he complained to Jodi. "Dolphins jumping all around, a big shark passing next to the boat. They scared away the fish."

Jodi, still excited and too impatient to spend time talking to Mero, quickly reassured him that he could fish as they headed in.

"I still can't believe it," she said breathlessly, after they were back in the boat. Mero, cruising slowly in a zigzag course, ignored them and prepared his lines. "When you told me what you saw yesterday, I couldn't help wondering if you had only imagined it. But now I've seen them, I've touched them . . . and I still find it difficult to believe. Do you think these are the only ones?"

"For all we know there are others out there, perhaps guarded by other schools of dolphins. Or maybe there were others and they didn't survive. We may never know."

"And those dolphins, Jim. So protective, not only of those four creatures, but of us.   Did you see them ram that shark?"

Jodi's animated gesturing brought a smile to Jim's face. He suddenly noticed Mero staring, his curiosity aroused.

"Mero is wondering what we're talking about. Why don't you tell him the shark he saw passed very close to you. I don't want him to think we're excited because we saw something else."

Jodi turned to the fisherman. Her explanation brought a look of alarm to his face.

"Mero says it would be better if I let you go in the water by yourself," she said, looking at Jim and trying not to laugh. "Jim, remember what I said last night about your having taken a step past theory? Now I know it's true, everything you said, all that conjecture and hypothesis. And you have photos to prove it."

At that moment, Mero had two strikes and lunged from one line to the other. He handed a rod to Jim and they both reeled in tuna. A few moments later, there was a hit on the third rod. For the next half hour, Jim and Mero pulled in fish, Mero dancing gleefully between the rods.

While their rich harvest piled up on the deck, Jodi stared thoughtfully at the flopping bodies.

"Jim, are you going to tell Doctor Chambers about this?" she said, coming out of her reverie.

He handed his rod to Mero and turned toward Jodi. "What do you mean?"

"Are you going to tell her what we saw?"

"I have to. That's why I came here in the first place."

She nodded, then turned away.

"What's the matter?"

"Just thinking. I'll talk to you about it later. I should get back to the clinic."

She spoke to Mero and with obvious reluctance he placed his rods on the deck, then turned the boat in a wide circle in preparation for their return to Illetto. The roar of the motor precluded any further conversation.

After docking, Jim carried his diving gear up to Mero's hut. Jodi was already on the path to her hut and he hurried to catch up.

"Something is bothering you," he said, placing his hand on her arm as they reached the door.

She turned to him, then shook her head and looked away.

"I have to think this through. Let's talk about it tonight."

"Okay. I know you have to get to the clinic. Can you put a radio call through to Bikini before you go?"

She looked at him sharply, then walked inside. Jim followed and when she had made contact with Bikini station, he asked that a boat be sent the next morning and that they notify Doctor Chambers to make flight arrangements to Kwajalein. The message completed, he turned to say something to Jodi, but she was gone.

The afternoon dragged for Jim. He first stopped at Kel's store to buy some water, then walked to the southern side of the island. A few flat-bottomed canoes were in the lagoon, the voices of the men carrying across the water while, nearby, Marshallese children cavorted near the beach. Jim thought of his daughters, suddenly missing them intensely. In only two weeks they would be coming back to La Jolla for spring break. He wondered if he should tell them what he had seen in the waters off Illetto. And whether he should talk about Jodi. He knew they would be happy that there was a woman he cared for, but perhaps that was premature. He didn't really know how Jodi felt.

He walked aimlessly until he ended up back at his own hut behind Kel's store. Reclining on a mat, Jim thought about what they had seen that day, and about Jodi. He understood why she thought he might have imagined his first glimpse of the fish heads. Even after touching them, she said, she still found it difficult to believe. So did he. It was obvious, too, that something else was troubling her. He went over the possibilities: the half-human creatures; the shark; his going back to Kwajalein; his approaching departure for the States—any of these things, or all of them. Whatever it was, he hoped she would tell him that evening.

He wondered, too, if he was directly responsible for what he now perceived as Jodi's unhappiness. The only emotional intimacy he had had since Aiko's death was with his daughters. He knew how much he cared for Jodi, but was he actually creating a distance between them out of loyalty to Aiko?

And what was he going to tell Virginia Chambers? That was what Jodi had asked him. He would tell her the truth, of course. And then what? Any decisions would be out of his hands. She would report to her superiors and . . . Is that what's bothering Jodi? he thought suddenly. He hadn't really given any thought to it. He had only focused on finding the creatures. Now that he had proven their existence, what would happen? He could envision other scientists being sent out to confirm his report. Then what?

Wrestling with his thoughts, Jim hadn't noticed the time. He checked his watch. It was after six. He quickly followed the path to Jodi's hut, but she was not there. No fire had been started in the pit. It would be unusual for her to still be at the clinic, so he headed for the beach.

In the rapidly fading light, he could see her sitting at the water's edge, her back to him. Approaching quietly, he sat down next to her.

"I thought you weren't coming," she said, not looking up.

"I lost track of time."

"There was a radio message for you a while ago. Bikini will have a boat here at eight tomorrow morning."

"Tell me what's troubling you, Jodi."

She clasped her drawn-up knees and threw a sideways glance at him. "I've been thinking about those creatures," she said, her voice flat. "When I first saw them, I was excited, but there was also a feeling of revulsion.

"We've all seen paintings of satyrs and mermaids, but we know those are fictions, things created by human imagination. These dolphin-like humans are real, created by human beings—with radiation.

"And then, watching the dolphins fight off the shark to protect those, to me, hideous creatures, I felt ashamed. The dolphins instinctively did what was right. Would human beings have put themselves at risk for creatures that were deformed or different? It was something . . . Noble, I guess, is the best word.

"After the shark had gone and those things were swimming around us, wanting so much to be touched, I no longer felt repelled. They seemed so vulnerable, so in need of protection.

"When we were back in the boat, I began to think about what would happen if you tell the people in Kwaj about this." She swung around to face him. "I think it would open a Pandora's box. At best, they'd try to capture one of these things for their so-called scientific studies; at worst . . . "

"You don't want me to tell them?"

"Jim, there are only four people who know anything about this. Mero will never say anything. He just wants to forget it."

"And Doctor Chambers?"

"If you tell her you didn't find anything, isn't it possible she'd be willing to forget all this?"

"She still has those parts in her refrigerator. And she operates by the book. She'll send them on to her superiors and they'll draw their own conclusions. There'll be other people here investigating and even if you don't tell them anything, they'll find out it was Mero who brought you the parts. He's the only one on the island with an outboard, don't forget. Sooner or later they'll find the creatures, just as we did."

Jodi looked at him earnestly. "But what if you could convince her? You could say it was an isolated mutant, something not worth the expenditure of time and effort."

"Jodi, you've met Virginia Chambers. Do you really think I can convince her of that?" He shook his head. "It wouldn't surprise me if she already contacted her superiors at the Department of Energy."

"I thought she had no intention of doing anything until you got back."

"I admit I don't know her that well. There were times in the past when I thought her heart was in the right place, but then I always had to remind myself that she's not just a physician. She's also an Army officer. That means she thinks of covering her own rear. Even if she hasn't done anything yet, I don't think I could convince her to drop the matter.

"And there are other things for you to consider. Shouldn't the world know about this? People have become so complacent about nuclear energy. Seeing this grotesque effect of radiation would shatter that complacency, make them realize there's a price to be paid. And it would make me uncomfortable to lie. That's just not the way I operate."

"I don't like lying either," she flashed. "But hasn't our government deceived the Marshallese? Wasn't it a lie to ignore the exposure on Illetto, to turn these people into an experiment without their knowledge?"

"I'm not disputing that—and I'm not excusing it. I'm only saying I don't like lying."

" I don't want you to do anything that will compromise what you believe in. I'm also not forgetting that it was I who took the parts to Doctor Chambers. But I wish you would, well, just not be forthcoming with her. Those things aren't hurting any one. I'd like to see them left in peace."

"I don't want to see them hurt any more than you do. But I can't make promises I don't know if I can keep.

"I've got to think about this, Jodi. I'll be back in a day or two, I hope, and then we can talk. I'll leave my gear at Mero's."

By now the wind had picked up, covering them with a fine shower of sand and spray. Dark clouds covered the gibbous moon and a gentle rain began to fall. They stood up, facing one another in the darkness.

"I can't make promises I can't keep either," said Jodi, an edge in her voice. "Have a good trip back to Kwaj."

A sudden chill passed through him as Jodi disappeared up the path. He heard the door of her hut open and close. Not since Aiko's death had he felt so alone.

NINE

Jim Newell eased into the second-floor conference room in Kwajalein Hospital just as Virginia Chambers began her lecture. Seated around a table were the three American physicians who worked full-time at the hospital; a group of nurses from two hospitals, Kwajalein and Ebeye; two Ebeye Hospital physicians; and three volunteer American physicians, there for short-term stays of two weeks.

Doctor Chambers paused, smiled briefly and nodded as Jim entered. "This is Doctor Newell," she said to the group. "Some of you probably already know him. He's worked here several times in the past as a volunteer and is now doing some research for us. Let's go around the table and introduce ourselves for his benefit."

The volunteers included an internist, a radiologist, and a gynecologist, two of them currently serving with the U.S. Army. They were assisting Doctor Chambers in follow-up examinations on patients exposed to fallout in 1954 on Rongelap, Utrik and Ailinginae, and on a control group of Marshallese.

Jim noticed that the nurses from Kwajalein's hospital were Americans, and that those from Ebeye were all Filipinos, as were the two physicians from that hospital. To his knowledge, there was only one Marshallese physician on Ebeye.

Noon conferences at Kwajalein were a tradition whenever Haverbrook Laboratory personnel made their semiannual visit. New volunteer physicians were expected to lecture on a subject in their field. The talk giving the background to Haverbrook's involvement with the Marshalls was always given by Doctor Chambers. It was one Jim had heard the last time he worked on Kwajalein.

The Department of Energy, she informed the group, was known as the Atomic Energy Commission at the time of the H-Bomb testing. It had contracted with Haverbrook after the Bravo blast to have physicians under Haverbrook's aegis follow all islanders known to have been exposed to radiation. Chambers, in her lecture, focused on thyroid abnormalities and thyroid cancer which, she claimed, were the only conditions directly attributable to the radiation exposure.

As she detailed the amounts of radioactive iodine picked up by thyroid glands in different age groups and presented the World Health Organization classification of thyroid disease, Jim was struck by what was not said: no mention of leukemia, known to be linked to radiation exposure in childhood; no reference to the high incidence of cataract formation in the exposed population; no mention of fallout as a possible contributing factor to the extraordinary number of cases of diabetes. And most important, abnormal births, especially those the Marshallese referred to as jellyfish babies, were not discussed at all.

The Americans, Jim knew, always denied the existence of those hideously deformed creatures that the Marshallese claimed had been born after H-Bomb Bravo and then immediately buried or thrown into the sea.

He wondered what the reaction of the doctors and nurses in this room would be if he were to tell them what he had discovered in the waters off Illetto, or if they could see what was in Doctor Chambers' refrigerator.

During the question period, Jim raised his hand.

"I just wanted to elaborate a bit on the Bravo shot so our new arrivals can understand the magnitude of what happened. The fireball from that blast was three miles in diameter. The crater it made in the reef was more than a mile wide and two hundred feet deep. The atomic cloud after the explosion rose to an altitude of more than twenty miles! As Doctor Chambers mentioned, the wind shift caused heavy contamination within a large area. The Japanese fishing vessel that was covered with fallout was outside the eighty-mile radius of what was considered the danger zone. One report stated that radiation exposure from fallout was rampant throughout the northern Marshall Islands, more in some places, less in others.

"That brings up another point. With all that radiation exposure, Doctor Chambers, you never mentioned abnormal births and genetic effects. What happened to women who were pregnant and exposed?"

Virginia Chambers' frozen smile appeared, then vanished. Her eyes stared directly at him and Jim could feel the anger.

"Naturally that was studied. Except for concentration of radioactive iodine in the fetal thyroid, which I've already mentioned, we've found nothing attributable to radiation from Bravo. All the reports of abnormal births received in the forty years of follow-up on exposed individuals are considered to be anecdotal."

Jim raised an eyebrow as he returned her stare. That's some anecdote in your refrigerator, he thought.

Doctor Chambers turned from him to field a question from one of the Filipino nurses. The young woman was shy and her voice barely audible.

"You'll have to speak up, my dear. We can't hear you."

"We have heard reports in Ebeye," she said, "that the United States intentionally allowed the Marshallese to be contaminated so they could be used as guinea pigs. It was to help the U.S. develop the capability to treat Americans in case the United States was exposed to radiation in a nuclear war. Can you comment on that, please."

"That's preposterous," said Chambers. "The American government would never permit people to be used as guinea pigs."

Jim closed his eyes and bit his tongue. If there was one thing he did not want, it was an altercation with Virginia Chambers. And there was no denying her ability to lie with a straight face.

She came up to him after the conference, her rigid smile in place. "Trying to put me on a spot, Doctor Newell?"

"You know I wouldn't do that, Virginia," he said ingenuously. "I only thought some of the others might be wondering about fetal or genetic effects, so I thought I'd clear the air."

"How was your trip?"

"Fine. Anything new here?"

"Did Bikini tell you I called?"

"Yes, but since I had nothing to report then, I thought I would wait to see you in person."

"Let's continue this in my office, shall we?"

She closed the door behind them.

"And you do have something to report now?" she said, sitting behind her desk and motioning toward the other chair.

Still troubled by the confrontation with Jodi, Jim hesitated. During his flight to Kwaj, he had replayed their conversation in his mind over and over. At first, he was sure his stand was the correct one. But now, enough doubts had surfaced to make him cautious. "Perhaps," he replied.

She looked at him quizzically. "I don't follow you."

"Have you told anyone about what's in your refrigerator?"

Doctor Chambers' face colored and she looked away. The silence confirmed Jim's fears.

"Who else knows?"

"It was a stupid oversight on my part, I'm afraid. That X-ray of the arm we made—I left the film lying on my desk. Chet Lovell, an internist from Fort Benning, came to my office to discuss something with me. He's one of the volunteer physicians you met at the conference. I wasn't here when he arrived and he picked up the film. He spotted the webbing between the fingers and noticed there was no name or date on the film. He was curious."

"What did you tell him?"

"I didn't really tell him anything. Actually, I ignored his questions and steered the conversation into the thyroid problems we'd seen during the past three weeks. But . . ."

"But?"

"But he suddenly asked me if the webbed fingers in the film had anything to do with fallout exposure. And he asked who the patient was. It put me in a difficult position. I didn't want him to think I was trying to conceal information. So I told him it was something you and I were investigating and that I hoped to learn more when you returned from Illetto."

"Did that explanation satisfy him?"

"I'm afraid not."

"What do you mean?"

"He apparently communicated with his chief of service at Benning. Yesterday I got a call from the Department of Energy. The Energy Secretary was contacted by the Surgeon General. The upshot is that we're going to have a visitor. He's arriving tomorrow."

"Who is it?"

"A Colonel Lothar Bohm. All I know is he's connected somehow with DOE and works at Walter Reed. He was vacationing in Hawaii when he was ordered to come here. I was supposed to be heading back to Boston the end of this week, but DOE is now insisting I stay here and extend whatever assistance I can to this colonel. And that means I'll have to show him the arm and head. They won't be very happy when they discover I've been sitting on this for several days."

Seeing her worried expression, Jim couldn't help feeling a little sorry for her.

"What did you find on Illetto?"

"There are more of these creatures."

Doctor Chambers' eyes opened wide. "You saw them?"

"Yes. We saw four of them."

"We?"

"Doctor Larsen and I."

"You were actually close enough to see them? You don't think you could be mistaken?"

"Virginia, we touched them. I have photographs."

"Jesus!"

"They were with a school of dolphins. I saw them on two different occasions. The first time I couldn't get close. But the second time they came right up to us. The dolphins were protecting them."

Doctor Chambers drummed her fingers nervously on the desk. "That means there may be even more of these things out there. It's hard to believe."

"Yes, there may be others. I don't think they're capable of surviving without dolphin protection, but who knows how many are protected by other schools. One thing we did find out is that three abnormal babies were born to Marshallese women who were early in their pregnancies and on Illetto during the Bravo blast. The natives told us they were born with fish heads, so they threw them into the sea. The Marshallese never made the connection with radiation exposure and banished the three women to another island. They lived there alone until they died."

"And you believe those abnormal babies survived?"

"I can't think of any other explanation. Not only did they survive, but they've managed to procreate. And now they're obviously evolving into creatures better able to survive underwater."

"I can't even begin to imagine what the repercussions of this will be. When DOE finds out . . . "

"That's what troubles me. When I first saw these half-human monstrosities, I was angry. It was our testing that was responsible. We had played with forces that we didn't adequately understand and the Marshallese were the ones who had suffered. All I could think of was getting the news out so governments could no longer downplay the longterm effects of nuclear radiation. I thought about Chernobyl and Three Mile Island. To most people these were abstractions that didn't warrant the closing down of all nuclear reactors. Just as one little girl, Anne Frank, personified the Holocaust in a way that people could relate to, I imagined using these half-human, half-dolphin creatures to make the world understand the dangers of nuclear power.

"Then I thought about it some more. And now I'm not so sure."

Doctor Chambers, her arms folded across her chest, said nothing, but watched Jim's face intently. He blinked rapidly, trying to put his thoughts into words.

"The genie is out of the bottle and we can't put it back in. These things that we created exist. But they're not hurting anyone. If anything, they're as gentle as the dolphins with whom they live. Jodi—Doctor Larsen—explained it well. She said that when she first looked at them, she felt only revulsion. But then she realized how gentle and vulnerable they were. At that point, she only wanted to protect them. I'm beginning to think she's right. If word gets out about their existence, I fear for their survival."

"Well then, you might say we're caught on the horns of a dilemma. But surely you're not proposing that we try to cover up what you've found?"

"Let's just say I don't think we should be very forthcoming. At least, not immediately."

"But you know when this Colonel Bohm sees what's in the refrigerator, it's bound to lead to an investigation."

"Why don't we just wait and see who—or what—we're dealing with. You say he's arriving tomorrow so we won't have long to wait."

"When were you planning to go back to California?"

"I'm not sure. I want to see what's going to come of this colonel's visit. And I have to go back to Illetto to pick up my gear."

She nodded and, as an afterthought, asked, "How did you like Doctor Larsen?"

Jim hoped his face did not reveal the consternation he felt. "Oh, she's very nice and a very competent physician. We, uh, hit it off quite well."

A slight smile played around Doctor Chambers' face. "I'm glad to hear that. Well, Colonel Bohm's flight gets into Kwaj at about two tomorrow afternoon, so it looks like you'll have some leisure time."

"I'll probably bicycle over to Emon Beach for a swim this afternoon."

"Will you join me at the club this evening for dinner?"

"I'd like that. We can talk more about strategy for tomorrow."

As he left the hospital, Jim was preoccupied with all he had heard. On Illetto, when he had expressed his fears to Jodi that Chambers would divulge Mero Attri's find to DOE personnel, he had not expected immediate involvement from the Secretary of Energy and Surgeon General. There was always the possibility that the colonel from Walter Reed would not set up an investigation, but that was something Jim would not have bet on.

Bicycling to the lodge, he thought of placing a radio call to Jodi, then decided to wait until after his meeting with Bohm. He knew he'd have to be circumspect about anything he'd say during the call, but he hoped he could put things right between them. More than anything, he just wanted to hear her voice.

TEN

"**Come** in, Doctor Newell," said Virginia Chambers, quickly closing the door behind him and locking it.

The arm and dolphin head were on the table and leaning over them, his hands planted on the table surface, was Colonel Lothar Bohm. This man with a gray crewcut did not look up until Doctor Chambers interrupted him for an introduction.

The two men shook hands, the colonel appraising Jim with pale blue eyes. He was tall, about the same height as Jim Newell, and Jim guessed he was in his late forties or early fifties. Although he usually avoided making snap judgements about people, Newell found himself troubled by the lack of warmth in Bohm's eyes. And not even the tanned skin and flowered Hawaiian shirt could soften the hard lines around his thin lips.

Shifting his attention, Jim noticed that the arm and head were more dessicated than the last time. An unmistakable odor of decay filled the room.

"They're not keeping well, even on ice," said Doctor Chambers nervously.

Ignoring her, Bohm turned to Jim. "I understand you and I share an interest in the genetic effects of radiation," said Bohm, seeming friendly.

"Are you a radiologist?" Jim asked.

"No. My training is in internal medicine and oncology. I've read several of your papers, Doctor Newell, and I heard you lecture at a conference in Chicago a few years ago. I admire your work so you can imagine what a pleasant surprise it was for me to discover you're here on Kwaj. Doctor Chambers tells me you've been in the Marshalls for a few days now so you've had some time to think about this amazing find." He motioned toward the table. "I'd be very interested to hear your thoughts."

"Doctor Chambers has obviously filled you in on why I'm here," replied Jim, still guarded, "so you have me at a disadvantage. I only know you're at Walter Reed. Mind telling me why you were selected to look into this."

"Of course. DOE has often used me as a consultant because of my work at Reed. Over the years, we've had women referred to us who had undergone radiation therapy for malignancies while pregnant. In some cases, their pregnancy was not discovered until after therapy had begun. That may surprise you, but you have to remember that some base hospitals don't adhere to the high standards of Walter Reed. Also, the sensitivity of pregnancy tests in past years wasn't what it is today. In other cases there was no alternative because of the extent of disease. A fair number of these women decided to continue with their pregnancies and we were particularly interested in the risk of genetic damage."

"And what have your studies shown? I don't recall seeing any reports in the literature."

"We're trying to accumulate more cases before publishing the data. But there were no surprises. Some cases of leukemia and some new malignancies that may or may not have been secondary to the radiation. And, of course, some fetuses were so severely damaged that they were stillborn or spontaneously aborted. But there was no evidence of genetic damage that could be passed down and we certainly never found anything like this."

"Do I understand that you're assuming that this is a genetic effect of radiation?" asked Jim, stressing the word assuming. "It could be an isolated mutation."

A hint of derision creased the colonel's lips.

"You don't really believe that, Doctor Newell." Bohm spoke as if sharing a joke. "I know you've been to Illetto where these parts were found. We're fully aware that Illetto was subjected to heavy fallout during Bravo. Obviously you went to find out if there were more of these partially human creatures. I'm simply interested in knowing what you found."

For a moment, Jim debated with himself. This man was a fellow physician, ostensibly in the Marshalls for the same reason he was. In that case, Jim was obligated to tell him. But he was put off by Bohm. Not even the disarming nature of his questions overcame Jim's distrust. That, along with Jodi's fears, decided him.

He shrugged. "Nothing really. What you see here is all we've got."

Virginia Chambers fidgeted, clicking a ballpoint pen and chewing her lower lip as she watched the two men. Finally, to Jim's relief, she sat down. He wondered if Bohm had picked up on her nervousness.

"Doctor Chambers tells me you're an accomplished scuba diver. You saw nothing out of the ordinary?"

"Tropical fish. A tiger shark. The usual."

"I share your interest. I'm going to Illetto to do some diving myself. Who knows, perhaps I'll have better luck." He stepped from behind the table and approached Jim. "But to be frank, Doctor Newell, I hope you and I could work together. I intend to be honest with you and I'd like to think you'll take me into your confidence. What we have on this table is so important that I'm going to put in a call to Energy Secretary Raymond and to Harold Mapes, the Surgeon General. They're responsible for my being here, as I'm sure Doctor Chambers informed you. These specimens will be flown out today to the Armed Forces Institute of Pathology and we'll probably he having visitors from Washington within the next few days. We're counting on you and Doctor Chambers to assist us in our investigation."

"I don't know if I can," said Jim. "I have to get back to my hospital."

"I told you I'm going to be completely up front with you, Doctor Newell. I took the liberty before leaving Hawaii of talking to the medical director at your hospital in La Jolla, a Doctor Knowles, and also with the administrator. They understand this to be a national security issue and expect you to do all you can to help us."

Jim blinked. "That was presumptuous on your part, wasn't it? And calling this business a national security issue is an exaggeration, wouldn't you say?"

There was a flash of anger in Lothar Bohm's response. "You don't really think this is simply a medical issue, do you? You've been to the Marshalls before. You know how important a base this is for our country's security. The political ramifications of what's lying on this table are potentially disastrous. Doctor Chambers' stay has already been extended by DOE. I hate to sound pompous by spouting phrases like patriotic duty, but I know you'd like to do what's best for your country. I also know you're volunteering your time here so I can't actually order you to stay and help us. Doctor Chambers would never have asked for your assistance if you weren't an expert. With your help, I'm sure we can conclude our investigation quickly and expedite your return to La Jolla."

Turning abruptly as if the whole matter was settled, Bohm directed his attention to Virginia Chambers. "I'll help you prepare these for shipment. Then, after I make my calls to Washington, we can talk more about Illetto. And I would very much like to meet with you again today, Doctor Newell."

"DOE gave me my own trailer for quarters," said Doctor Chambers. "Why don't I prepare dinner for us tonight. We can talk in private there. You'll join us, won't you, Doctor Newell?"

Jim would have liked to forget that Lothar Bohm existed, but he could not ignore the pleading tone in Chambers' invitation. And he certainly wanted to be in on Bohm's intentions. They would meet at six. In the meantime, Jim had his calls to make.

After bicycling to the lodge, he purchased vouchers that allowed him to make personal calls, all routed through Hawaii. Jim thumbed through his address book, so cluttered with names and numbers that the alphabetical index was almost useless. He spotted the name he wanted—Mark Cantwell.

Cantwell was an internist from Saint Louis and a past president of the American Medical Association. They had met three years earlier in Cozumel when both were on a diving holiday. Although Cantwell was at least fifteen years older, and very involved with medical politics, the two men had hit it off, scuba diving providing the bond that cemented their friendship. They had kept in touch, often talking of doing a Red Sea diving trip, but were never able to coordinate the time away from their busy schedules.

"Don't tell me," said Cantwell when he heard Jim's voice. "Is it finally going to happen?"

Jim laughed. "Not yet, Mark, but I haven't forgotten. I'm calling you from the Marshall Islands."

"You lucky devil. How's the diving?"

"Well, this isn't a vacation. I'm here in a research capacity and the diving has been for that. When I get back to California I'll tell you about it. I'm calling to ask a favor. Have you ever heard of an internist at Walter Reed named Lothar Bohm?"

"Bohm? I know I've heard that name but I can't place it. Is he someone I should know?"

"Not really. But I think it would be helpful to me if I knew something about his background. He does oncology at Reed and says he has a particular interest in the genetic effects of radiation exposure."

"Hmm. Sounds like you two have something in common. How soon do you need this information?"

"As soon as possible. I know it's an imposition."

"How can I reach you?"

"I'm staying at the lodge for transients on Kwajalein. Here's the number."

"How much longer will you be there?"

"I wish I knew. I had hoped to be back in La Jolla before the end of the week but things are up in the air. I'm sorry I can't go into it now."

"Sounds a little mysterious. Are you there on your own?"

"No, it's a Department of Energy matter."

"I see. Well, no more questions then. I'll do what I can and get back to you."

Jim then went to the billeting office desk to see about putting through a radio call to Illetto. He was directed to another building. Being on a base less than a mile and a half in area and on flat terrain has its advantages, thought Jim, heading out to make his call. By now it was five o'clock but everything on the island was only minutes away, an advantage when bicycling in tropical heat. He felt ill at ease about having dinner with Bohm but hoped that talking to Jodi would lift his spirits.

"It's good to hear you," he said.

"Likewise. I hoped you'd call. How is everything?"

"Could be better," he said cautiously, knowing these calls were easily monitored.

"What we discussed has taken place," he said, hoping she understood his veiled reference to Doctor Chambers revealing the existence of the arm and dolphin head. "I'll be at a meeting tonight and hope to learn more.

"Are you there?" he asked, when there was no reply.

"Yes. Sorry. Any idea when you'll be returning?"

"No, afraid not. I hope soon."

"Me, too. Take care of yourself.'

After they hung up, Jim was filled with a sense of frustration at not being able to speak openly. He returned to the lodge planning to call his daughters but decided against it. Jill and Meredith were too attuned to his moods and his sour disposition would only worry them.

After a fast shower, he bicycled slowly toward Virginia Chambers' trailer.

What was it, he asked himself, that he particularly disliked about Lothar Bohm? He didn't really know the man and on the surface their meeting had been cordial, at least until that unpleasantness at the end. Bohm was a physician, but he was also a career military officer, which might account for some of his behavior. He appeared dedicated to his work and, judging from what he said, to his country's interests. The man had not complained about having his vacation interrupted. But there was something, something Jim could not put his finger on, that made him uncomfortable.

He wondered if his wariness arose from Jodi's concern for the creatures. Perhaps Jodi was being unreasonable in expecting the worst from government personnel. But he couldn't deny the scientific community's role in the fallout that had covered Rongelap,Utrik and Ailinginae. Even if that had been an accident, there was still Illetto.

Bohm himself had mentioned the radioactive contamination there, a danger intentionally kept from the Marshallese government.

Swinging off his bike in front of Doctor Chambers' trailer, he decided to keep an open mind. He would listen to what Bohm had to say and then make up his mind about how forthcoming to be and how much cooperation he would give.

"Come in, Doctor Newell," Chambers called out as he knocked.

The smell of roasting chicken greeted him as he entered. Lothar Bohm was already seated in the living room and raised a glass of wine in greeting. Doctor Chambers, busy at a stove in the adjoining kitchen, turned briefly toward him.

"Pour yourself some wine. The bottle's on the table. Dinner is almost ready."

Jim poured a glass and took a seat opposite Bohm. The two sat in silence for a few moments until Doctor Chambers joined them.

"Well, let's eat, shall we?" Her smile was forced, tentative.

"It's certainly nice of you to do this, Virginia," said Jim. "It smells wonderful."

"Yes, well, eating at the club gets tiresome after a while. Now that most of the patients have been seen, I can unwind a bit, although the statistical work keeps us almost as busy as the clinical work."

To cover her nervousness, she talked rapidly about examinations of the past weeks, giving extensive details of cases that had interested her. It was, Jim thought, as if she were trying to put off discussing what was uppermost in their minds. The two men listened politely until finally Bohm found an opportunity to interrupt.

"I have some news for you," he said quickly, looking from one to the other. "I spoke to Secretary Raymond and Surgeon General Mapes. Secretary Raymond will be flying out from Washington tonight. The Surgeon General is on his way to a conference in Brussels, but he's sending his aide, Doctor Amos Whittier. Doctor Whittier will leave Washington first thing in the morning. We can expect them both day after tomorrow."

"And you've sent the specimens to Washington?" asked Jim.

Bohm looked at his watch. "They left fifteen minutes ago on the flight to Honolulu. They should be with the Institute pathologists tomorrow evening."

"Then our visitors won't be able to see the...."

"We have photographs and a detailed description for them," interrupted Bohm. "And we have the X-rays."

"What do you think they'll propose?"

Bohm sipped his wine, staring over his glass at Jim. "They'll want to meet with you and Doctor Chambers first, of course. And then at some point they'll want to talk to the other doctor." He turned to Chambers. "The one on Illetto. What was her name—Larsen?"

Jim looked down at his plate to avoid Bohm's eyes. So Chambers has told him about Jodi, too, he thought bitterly, and that means he probably knows about Mero Attri.

"And after the meeting?" Jim asked, seeming to concentrate on buttering a slice of bread.

"Head out to Illetto. Any accomodations there?"

"If any are available, I think they'll be a little primitive for your visitors. It would mean sleeping on floor mats."

"There's a way around that. I have an appointment tomorrow morning with a Major Andrews in the transportation section here. There's a large boat moored at the base on Roi-Namur. They use it for visiting brass. Sleeps eight and has modern conveniences. Andrews is sure he can get it for us. How much diving gear do you have with you?"

"Only my own. It's still on Illetto."

Bohm turned toward Doctor Chambers. "Perhaps you can make some inquiries about gear for two or three people in the morning. Let me know by noon if it poses a problem. If it does, that will give me time to make arrangements to have it brought from Honolulu."

The man is thorough, thought Jim. And determined.

"How will you decide where to dive?" Jim asked, wishing he could take the words back.

Bohm's impassive blue eyes stared into Jim's face. "How did you decide?"

Jim's shrug was met with a sneer impersonating a smile.

"I think," said Bohm, "that since we're dealing with a creature that's obviously an air-breathing mammal, I'd look for dolphin schools. And I'd arrange for the fisherman who hit the thing to take us to the spot where it happened. But I'm sure that's what you did, too."

They sat in silence as he awaited confirmation. There was a flicker of annoyance around his eyes when Jim made no response.

"Are we ready for dessert and coffee?" asked Doctor Chambers, trying to break the tension.

"None for me, thank you," said Bohm.

"If you're planning to have some," Jim said, "I'll join you."

As she got up, Jim's thoughts raced. If he could get to Illetto by tomorrow and tell Jodi what was happening, they would be able to get off the island before Bohm and his visitors arrived. That would avoid their pressuring her for information. It would also give them a chance to talk to Mero Attri.

He turned to Bohm. "You seem to have everything planned very well so I don't suppose you'll be needing me any further. I'd like to get back to Illetto, pick up my gear and head back to the States."

"On the contrary, Doctor Newell." He shook his head and smiled humorlessly, as if dealing with a forgetful schoolboy. "I thought we'd decided all that earlier. Secretary Raymond and Doctor Whittier are looking forward to meeting you. They think you can be very helpful. Captain Anderson at Scripps has told us what a fine diver you are. Surely you can't object to a few extra days of diving before getting back to work."

So he's talked to Scripps about me, too, thought Jim, feeling violated. Keeping an open mind was proving to be more difficult than he had anticipated. He hoped Mark Cantwell's inquiries about Bohm would help him reciprocate.

"I take it then," said Jim, "that if the visitors from Washington arrive on Thursday, you'll plan to be on Illetto by Friday."

"Or Saturday at the latest, if we can have the boat from Roi-Namur in Bikini by then. But we'll be talking before that. If our visitors don't run into any travel delays, we'll probably be meeting on Thursday evening. Doctor Chambers will keep you posted."

After coffee, the two men stood and thanked her for dinner. As they headed for their bicycles, Bohm cast a sideways glance at Jim.

"I admire a man who keeps his own counsel," he said. "But there are times, especially when important matters are at stake, that it's better to share information. Goodnight, Doctor Newell."

Jim turned and headed for the club. He didn't feel like having a drink but he certainly didn't want to bicycle to the lodge with Bohm. Once again, he found himself thinking about his antipathy to this man. It was out of character to take such an immediate dislike to someone he barely knew. But, even when Bohm seemed to take Jim into his confidence, there was a hint of menace behind it. What particularly worried him was how much pressure Bohm would attempt to put on Jodi. He didn't know how much influence Bohm had in Washington, but since Jodi still had another year to serve with the U.S. Public Health Service he did not want the man to cause difficulties for her.

Instead of stopping at the club, Jim headed for the dock where the launch left for Ebeye. He stared at the reflected lights in the water and thought of Jodi. He knew now that he would not see her until Friday or Saturday, but he would have to alert her before then. He decided to put a call through after his meeting on Thursday.

Jim's phone was ringing as he entered his room. He was surprised to hear Mark Cantwell's voice.

"Mark, I didn't expect to hear from you so soon."

"Well, I found out a few things that might interest you. Your man is an oncologist at Reed and well thought of by his colleagues—professionally, at least. He has the reputation of being a martinet. Nothing wrong with that, I suppose, but words like cold and demanding crop up when you talk to people. Attended good schools—Georgetown for undergrad, Rochester Med School, internship and residency in internal medicine at Henry Ford, then oncology training at Mass General. Uncle Sam paid for his education and he began active military service after finishing at Mass General. He's got twenty years under his belt. One of my sources thought he'd be coming up shortly for a promotion to general."

"I'd have to agree about his personality but the rest of it sounds fine. No skeletons in the closet, then."

"Skeletons, you said? You may have chosen the right word. Bohm has published quite a bit. Some articles on genetic effects of radiation were no surprise since you told me that was an interest of his."

"It's odd that I haven't come across his work."

"Well, most of it was published in military journals. But there were some articles that caught my eye. *The Immune Response to Torture*, co-authored with some Chilean MD. Bohm apparently spent time there during the Pinochet regime. Other articles had such intriguing titles as *Lymphocytic Response to Lethal Injection in Rhesus Monkeys* and *The Effects of Carbon Monoxide Poisoning on Leukemic Blast Cells*. This guy sounds like a million laughs. Anyway, subjects like those piqued my interest. So I did something that wasn't quite above board."

"Should I sit down, Mark?"

"I think you can handle this on your feet. I have a friend, someone of importance who shall be nameless. Lots of connections, access to files and security clearances, that sort of thing. This friend came up with something interesting but I must have your word this information will remain confidential. I hope to hell, too, this phone line isn't being monitored."

"I can't vouch for the phone line, but I give you my word. And we're not exactly discussing state secrets. So what can anyone do? Shake a finger at us?"

"Well, here it is then. Bohm became chief of oncology at Reed about six years ago. His predecessor was a man named John Hatfield. Hatfield died in an accident and Bohm was then appointed."

"I don't understand, Mark. Am I supposed to infer something from that?"

"Did you know that Bohm shares our passion for diving?"

"Yes, he told me. In fact, he wants me to go with him on some dives."

There was silence on the other end.

"Are you there, Mark?"

"Yes. Look, I told you Hatfield died in an accident. He and Bohm were diving together when it happened."

"What?"

"They were both in Hawaii, some sort of military junket. Bohm's version was that they got separated while exploring an underwater wreck. Other divers went down to search for Hatfield and they found his body inside the wreck. The sharks had already been at him but there was never any explanation about how he had died."

"Surely you don't think . . . "

"The military conducted an investigation. Bohm seemed very upset about what had happened, even said he blamed himself for not sticking closer to Hatfield. Anyway, they concluded it was an accidental death, possibly due to a shark attack while he was alive. Bohm was cleared of any involvement. One month later he had Hatfield's job."

"I don't think we can draw any...."

"Jim, I'm not saying it wasn't an accident. I just find it an interesting coincidence. And one more thing. Don't invite him along for our Red Sea trip."

Jim laughed. "I really appreciate your getting this information for me, Mark. All in all I'd have to say our man checks out okay."

"Yeah," said Cantwell. "But do me one favor, Jim."

"What's that?"

"I don't know what you're involved in there but—just be careful."

"I'll do that. And if we ever manage to pull off the Red Sea dive, I'll pick up the tab for dinner and drinks. Thanks again, Mark."

That night, not wanting to run into Bohm, Jim avoided the club. Instead, he walked over to the fields fronting Ocean Road and watched a softball game. When the game ended, he walked slowly north along the beach, his thoughts still very much on Mark Cantwell's call. As disquieting as that information was, he had to discount any involvement by Bohm in his diving partner's death. After all, he had been cleared in the investigation and he had been upset enough, from what Mark said, to blame himself. Accidents did happen during dives. He had his own scars to remind him of that. And as for the subject of some of Bohm's published papers, perhaps that was to be expected when doing research for the military. It didn't necessarily mean there was a macabre side to Bohm.

Jim reminded himself, too, that Bohm was only one player on the team that was coming to the Marshalls, and certainly a subordinate one. Perhaps he would be able to establish better rapport with the new arrivals. But Jim was forced to admit that he would have to keep his guard up.

He stopped at a ramada along the beach. A group of Marshallese were partying and Jim recognized some who worked at the hospital. One man, an orderly, motioned to him. He joined them at one of the tables and the man reached into an ice chest and handed him a beer. On a small raised platform at the end of the thatched building, a man began to strum a guitar. To the applause of the crowd, a young Marshallese woman danced a hula, her arms moving sinuously and her hips swaying to the music.

The tropical night was filled with music and the gentle sound of surf breaking on the beach. Jim, suddenly weary, closed his eyes. For what seemed like a brief moment, he dozed, awakening with a start. It was late. The music and dancing had stopped and the Marshallese were drifting away. Jim slowly stood and followed the stragglers to the road.

A lone bicyclist was heading toward the lodge. Jim, walking in the same direction, turned to look at him as he passed.

The man, his face a ghastly waxen color in the glow of the street lights, showed no sign of recognition. The prickling at the base of Jim's scalp told him it was Lothar Bohm.

ELEVEN

An early riser, Jim appeared at the hospital right after breakfast to see if he could be of any help. Only three patients were on the ward, all diabetics recovering from below-the-knee amputations for gangrene. He visited with the physician on duty for a few minutes, then returned to his room and changed into a swimsuit. The pool was only a short walk from the lodge and after a half-hour of laps, Jim wondered what to do with the rest of the morning. Still irritated by Lothar Bohm's insistence that he stay on Kwajalein for the meeting, he snatched his towel from the deck chair and headed back to his room.

As he walked along Ocean Road, he heard his name called. Virginia Chambers was pedalling her bicycle toward him.

"Oh, Doctor Newell, I'm glad I found you. Something terrible has happened."

"Oh? What is it?"

"There was a radioed SOS from Illetto during the night. The person calling Bikini could barely speak English but from what they were able to understand, the doctor on the island is missing."

Jim was stunned. His lips formed Jodi's name, but he couldn't speak.

"They weren't sure if they understood correctly but the man who runs a store on the island said she had gone out on a boat the previous afternoon and hadn't returned. Bikini is sending one of their own boats and a spotter plane to try to find her."

"Virginia, I've got to get up there."

"But there's nothing you can do. They're looking for her. And we have that meeting tomorrow night."

"The hell with the meeting. I'm going to Illetto."

Jim's anger flared as she protested. "Goddammit, Virginia, I'm not in the Army and I'm not taking orders from anyone. I came here as a favor to you. If Bohm wants me to be at a meeting, he can have it in Illetto. All I care about right now is Jodi."

Doctor Chambers quickly placed a hand on his arm. "I'm sorry. I didn't know how you felt. I'll get you on a flight this morning. You should be on Illetto before evening. I'm sure they'll have found Doctor Larsen by then."

"Thanks, Virginia," Jim said, relieved. Call me at the lodge as soon as you have the flight time. I just can't understand what she . . . Well, I'd better run."

"Don't worry about the meeting. I'll tell Doctor Bohm you had an emergency."

Jim's heart pounded as he walked rapidly to the lodge. It must have been Mero Attri's boat, he thought, but why had she gone out again? Had there been another accident involving the creatures? What could have happened to the boat and to Jodi? If there had been a minor problem with the boat, Mero would have corrected it in a short time. He was too good a seaman and too meticulous with his boat and engine to imagine him having a more serious problem. That knowledge caused more anxiety. The irony of the situation wasn't lost on him. All these years of being alone, of believing that there would never be anyone who could replace Aiko. Was this chance for new happiness to be taken away from him?

Stop thinking the worst, he said to himself angrily as he stuffed his clothes into his bag. She'll be all right. She has to be. Suddenly, he jumped as the phone rang.

"You're on the next flight to Roi," said Virginia Chambers. "It leaves in forty minutes. You should just be able to make the connecting flight to Bikini. They know you're coming and will get you to Illetto."

"Thanks, Virginia. Any word on the search?"

"They've only just started."

"Okay. Thanks again."

The flights seemed an eternity for Jim. When he reached Bikini, the men at the base still had no news. Their boat was searching the waters around Illetto and they had heard nothing from the spotter plane.

As his craft neared the dock next to Mero Attri's house, Jim was surprised to find a small American military launch moored there.

Standing at the dock was the fisherman himself, a young sailor at his side. Both men were staring intently at Mero's boat which had been dragged on shore, a gaping hole beneath the bow.

"Where's Doctor Larsen?" Jim called out, leaping onto the dock.

A surprised look on Mero's face faded as he recognized Jim. He spoke rapidly in Kajin Majel, the language of the islands, and pointed at his boat.

"The doctor just headed for home," said the sailor. "She was all done in."

"What happened?" asked Jim, exhaling with relief.

"We got the radio message last night on Bikini that the boat hadn't returned. But by then it was too dark to begin searching. We waited for first light but the weather didn't cooperate. We had to wait until late morning to send the plane up. The pilot spotted the boat stuck on a reef about five miles northwest of Illletto. It was taking a pretty good pounding. I got out there as quickly as I could. The two of them were exhausted from baling all night but otherwise they're okay. They're certainly in better shape than the boat."

"I can't believe this happened," Jim said, looking at Mero. The fisherman's morose gaze was fixed on the torn frame of his fishing boat. "This guy knows the waters around here like the back of his hand."

"The doctor said they were pretty far out when the water got rough. His engine kept conking out and the waves drove them onto the reef. They kept hoping another boat would spot them, but when it got dark they knew they'd have to make the best of it. It's a good thing one of the guys here knew how to send an SOS. Another day's pounding by waves would have finished the boat."

Jim made a mental note to give Lekoj Kel a hug when he saw the man. He thanked the sailor and asked him to contact Doctor Chambers when he got back to Bikini.

Hurrying toward Jodi's hut, Jim felt almost lightheaded. He knocked gently on the door but received no response. Slowly pushing the door open, he entered to find Jodi on her cot, deep in sleep. Wet clothes were on the floor mat. She had changed into dry shorts and a tee shirt before collapsing. Jim decided not to awaken her. Gathering up her wet clothes, he slipped noiselessly from the hut and draped them on the thatched roof to dry.

The tropical green colors of Illetto had never appeared so vivid as Jim headed down the path to the island's store. Slumped in a chair, dozing in the late afternoon heat, Lekoj Kel jumped up as Jim entered, his face breaking into a broad smile.

Jim, throwing his arms around him, patted his back. "Thank you for calling Bikini," he said seriously.

"Doctor okay?" Kel asked, a look of concern on his face.

"Yes, Doctor Larsen is fine. Sleeping now."

Kel nodded. "Mero okay?"

"Mero is fine, too. But the boat . . . " Jim shook his head.

"Boat no okay?"

Jim, forming a circle with his fingers, tried to explain about the hole. He wasn't sure he'd been understood until the man made a clucking sound and said, "Mero no fish now."

"Not for a while; I'm afraid."

Kel pointed to his own chest. "I fix. I good." He made a hammering motion.

Jim smiled, then glanced at the shelves which were still meagerly stocked. He purchased canned sardines and vegetables, then picked bananas as he headed back along the path. The sky over the western end of the lagoon now had an orange glow and Jodi's house was cloaked in shadows. He slipped quietly into the hut. Her position on the cot hadn't changed.

He kneeled next to her and brushed away some strands of hair that had blown over her face. She stirred and moaned in her sleep. Opening her eyes, she stared at him in the dim light of the room.

"Jim, is it really you? Am I dreaming?"

"No. You're not dreaming."

She eased herself up and leaned back on her elbows. "But how? How did you get back so soon?"

"Bikini called Kwaj this morning to report that you were missing. I came right away."

"I'm sorry. I hope . . . But I'm glad you're here."

Still half-asleep, Jodi lay back and stretched out her arms to encircle Jim's neck. He leaned over and kissed her gently.

"If this is a dream, I'm not sure I want to wake up," she murmured with a smile.

"What were you doing out there, Jodi?" Jim said, suddenly serious.

She forced herself into a sitting position, stifling a yawn. "God, what a terrible night that was. Come, sit next to me."

With an embarrassed smile, she placed a hand on his. "I know it was foolish but after I spoke to you the other evening, even though you couldn't tell me what was happening I had the sense that—that we were being threatened, not us, but those creatures. I thought I would try to scare them away. Then maybe they wouldn't come back. I took a flare gun with me, thinking the noise and light would do the trick. But we never spotted them or the dolphins even though we covered the whole area. I didn't tell Mero what I planned.

"We were quite a way out when I decided we'd better head back. But by then the seas were getting rough. Mero's motor kept cutting out. A large wave caught us broadside while he was working on the engine and slammed us onto a reef. I lost my flare gun. Water gushed in through a hole in the hull. It was just as well we were pinned on the reef because the boat couldn't have stayed afloat for more than a few seconds.

"I was scared, but I kept telling myself someone would spot us. They had to, because . . . " She squeezed his hand.

Jim put his arm around her shoulders and she leaned her head against him. "Did the sailor tell you how they happened to be looking for you?"

"No. I could barely keep my eyes open while he brought us back."

"Kel managed to send an SOS to Bikini on your radio after Mero's wife alerted him that the boat hadn't returned."

"Oh, that wonderful man. It was only last week that I showed him how to send an SOS, just in case."

Jim laughed. "It's a good thing the student learned his lesson so well. That sailor said the boat wouldn't have held together much longer. I was surprised he towed the boat in."

"He wasn't going to but Mero pleaded with me. The boat is his livelihood, so what could I do? I convinced the sailor and we managed to get it off the reef. I don't remember much after that. All I wanted to do was sleep. Is it badly damaged?"

"A big hole. Kel told me he'd fix it."

"I'm sure he will. He put up his store by himself. I really feel bad for Mero. I'm responsible because I asked him to take me out. But tell me what's been happening on Kwaj."

"Let's eat first. Sorry I couldn't do any better than this," said Jim, showing her the cans and bananas.

"Anything is a feast right now."

As they ate, Jim told her about his meeting with Lothar Bohm and the impending arrival of Jeanne Raymond and Amos Whittier. He didn't mention Bohm's connection with the diving accident in which his predecessor had died.

"Well, that confirms all of your fears about Doctor Chambers. Does she know that we saw the creatures?"

"I told her. And she knows I have photographs. Bohm sent the specimens to the Armed Forces Institute of Pathology. I don't think Chambers has told him anything more. At least she hadn't when I left. But he knows about Mero and he knows Mero brought the parts to you."

"What will happen now?"

"Bohm was arranging for a VIP boat based in Roi to be taken to Bikini for them to live on. They'll meet it there and sail for Illetto, probably arriving here on Friday or Saturday. I know they'll want to meet with us and they'll probably ask Mero to show them where the accident happened."

"Does Bohm know about the dolphins?"

"He said he would look for dolphin schools. The man is smart, Jodi. He's also a scuba diver."

As Jodi's brow furrowed with worry, Jim tried to reassure her. "Look, no one knows better than you that you can be out there all day and not spot dolphins."

"Yes, but from what you say about Bohm, he doesn't sound like a man who'll give up easily. And if he does spot the same school, what do you think he'll do then?"

"I don't know. There's something about the man that makes me wary. He's smooth and outwardly friendly but at the same time he's calculating. I get the feeling he'll do anything to get what he wants. But there's no way to know how much influence he'll have on the others. One thing I'm sure of is they won't do anything while they're here. No one working for the government does anything on his own. If they spot the creatures, they'd probably have to clear their next move with Washington.

"While I was on Kwaj I thought of getting you off Illetto so we wouldn't be here when they arrived. But that would only convince them we were hiding something. The best thing is just to stay here and see what we're up against. I'm hoping that after we meet with them, we'll be able to judge what we should do next. After the scare you gave me no problem seems insurmountable."

Jodi smiled and quickly asked, "Did you tell Bohm that I speak the language here?"

"Chambers might have. What are you thinking?"

"If Bohm doesn't bring an interpreter, it will make things difficult for them. And I can ask Mero to stay clear of the area where he hit the creature and to try to avoid the dolphins."

"Won't Mero wonder why?"

"I can tell him we don't know what these people plan to do with the dolphins. The Marshallese believe the dolphins lead them to fish. They wouldn't want any harm to come to them. And remember, even though Mero knows you're here because of the thing he hit, he doesn't know what we saw under the surface."

"It's worth a try. And if they spot the dolphins anyway . . . "

"There's not much we can do about that. But if a few days go by and they don't find them, maybe they'll call it quits."

"You'll talk to Mero then?"

"First thing tomorrow. I want to give him some money anyway, to tide him over until the boat is repaired."

By now the last trace of color in the western sky had disappeared and the room was immersed in darkness.

"Shall I light the lamp?" asked Jodi.

"No. You're tired. You'll feel better after a good night's sleep."

"I feel badly about how we left things before you went to Kwaj." She held out her hand and Jim took it in his. "Will you come back in the morning?"

Jim suddenly remembered the pain he had felt when he lost Aiko, almost more than he could bear. He realized how devastated he would have been to lose Jodi as well.

"I'll be back," he said.

TWELVE

"Good morning. Sleep well?" Jim asked as he arrived shortly after sunrise. Jodi already had a fire going and water boiling for coffee.

"I owe you an apology," Jodi said as they headed for the beach with their coffee. "I'm sorry for the way we ended our talk that night before you left. I thought about it a lot. Your argument had as much merit as mine. I'm afraid I overreacted."

"I understood how you felt about protecting those creatures. In fact, I've come around to your way of thinking."

"I don't understand. Everything you said about making sure people were kept informed about the dangers of nuclear radiation was valid."

"I suppose so. But, as I explained to Doctor Chambers, what's done is done and now we have to live with the result. Meeting Bohm only reinforced that. I don't know what he'd do if he found those things. Anyway, I just want you to know we're on the same side."

Jodi stared at the coffee cup in her lap. "There's something else . . . " She raised her eyes to his. "I was happy to find you kneeling at my cot yesterday when I woke up. That you raced back to Illetto while all that business with Bohm was going on wasn't lost on me, no matter how sleepy I was. What I'm trying to say, Jim, is I'd like you to ignore what I said the other evening."

"And I have a confession to make," he said, laughing. "I had every intention of doing just that."

Later that morning, after Jodi had made her home visits, they took a swim and then walked on the beach. The hours sped by, surprising both of them when they noticed it was time for Jodi to open the clinic. That afternoon, after she had finished seeing patients, they visited

Mero Attri. Lekoj Kel was already hammering at the hull of the fishing boat while Mero was sawing on a plank.

The fisherman smiled as Jim and Jodi approached. "In only a few days, I will be fishing again, thanks to my good friend, Kel," he said animatedly.

"Looks like all of us owe a debt to Kel," said Jodi. "Did he tell you he was the one who got help for us?"

A look of surprise came over Mero's face and, suddenly serious, he turned to his friend, speaking softly. Kel made a gesture of dismissal, but Mero seemed deeply touched.

"He says he loves Kel like a brother," Jodi translated. Turning to Mero she said, "Please take this," as she handed him a twenty-dollar bill. "It will help until you can go fishing again."

Mero shook his head, saying it wasn't necessary, but Jodi insisted. With reluctance Mero took the money and thanked her.

Jodi turned to Jim and smiled. "He says the first fish he catches will be for us."

"Are you going to tell him about Bohm and the others?"

Taking the fisherman aside, Jodi alerted him about the situation. He listened attentively then asked a few questions.

"What did he say?"

"If any dolphins are sighted, it won't be because he tried to find them. He wanted to know if he could get in any trouble and I reassured him. You didn't mention the other island to Doctor Chambers, did you?"

"Yes, but I don't think she'll pass that on to Bohm. I got the feeling that she was uncomfortable with him, too."

"I hope she doesn't say anything. I wouldn't want Bohm asking Mero about it. The Marshallese aren't good at lying. You know, the first question a Marshallese will ask about someone he doesn't know is 'is he kind?' They have some interesting proverbs here, like 'kindness is living and meanness is death'. When I mentioned Bohm, Mero asked me if he was kind."

"How did you answer that one?"

"I told him I didn't know, that we would have to wait and see."

Jim gave a humorless laugh. "That was honest."

That evening, sitting around the fire after dinner, Jim and Jodi realized their relationship was past the point of simple friendship.

"I'm going to miss you when you leave," said Jodi.

Jim nodded. "I feel the same way. You've made me realize that for years I've only been going through the motions of living."

Later, as they said goodnight, Jim wrapped his arms around her and kissed her. Jodi gently gripped his shoulders and leaned into him. They stood for a long moment, Jodi's body pressed against his as they listened to the roar of the surf behind them. Then, suddenly shy, Jodi stood on tiptoe and planted a peck on his cheek. "I'd better go."

"Sleep well, Jodi," Jim replied softly, not moving until her door had closed behind her.

Shortly after dawn, they borrowed one of the Marshallese canoes and spent the morning exploring the lagoon. In the afternoon Jodi again saw a few patients and then they walked over to Mero Attri's dock. Mero proudly showed them Kel's completed work.

"I will take it out on the water tomorrow," he said. "The seal will be dry by then."

Later, they sat on the dock, watching for the boat as dusk descended.

When it was almost dark, Jodi gave a sigh of relief. "It looks like we have a reprieve."

As they walked back to Jodi's hut, Kel caught up to them, a package in his hands.

"My cousin from Ailinginae was here this morning," he said, offering the bundle. "He had good luck and brought more than enough fish for my family. I have some tuna steaks for you."

They thanked the storeowner and tried to pay him, but he laughed and hurried away.

"That's another reprieve," said Jim, from sardines for the third night in a row."

"And one of my patients brought me a papaya," said Jodi. "We'll have a feast."

That night, as they relaxed on the beach after dinner and watched the moon over the ocean, Jim put his arm around her. "I enjoy being with you, Jodi. It makes me wish time could stand still."

As they walked slowly back to the hut, neither willing to have the evening end, Jodi whispered, "I really want you to stay the night, Jim, but I don't know if I can trust myself."

Overwhelmed by feelings he had not experienced for years, Jim nodded. "Everything in its own time," he said, kissing her. With reluctance, they separated.

On Saturday morning they breakfasted on the beach, saying very little. Jodi then made her rounds while Jim walked around Illetto. Arriving at Mero's house, he scanned the water for any sign of the boat. It was almost noon when he spotted a white shape on the horizon, miles out. He watched as the boat's lines slowly became distinct.

Jodi suddenly appeared at his side. "I thought I'd find you here," she said. "Looks like our holiday is over."

They watched with a mixture of amazement and dread as the boat approached. This yacht was not what they had expected.

It looks right out of Newport-Balboa, Jim thought. "I guess it pays to be a VIP," he mumbled softly.

The boat had barely touched the pier when a sailor leaped onto Mero Attri's rickety dock and tied the bow fast. He was followed by a man of medium height with thinning blond hair. Although slender, there was no mistaking his strength as he caught a line thrown by the captain and pulled the boat's stern around to keep the vessel lined up along the pier.

Lothar Bohm was the next to step off. He waved to Jim, then turned his attention to the other passengers descending the ramp.

Jeanne Raymond, the Energy Secretary, was fiftyish, a short, stocky woman with closely cropped grey-blond hair. Her meticulously tailored linen skirt, white silk blouse and low-heeled pumps seemed out of place on a Pacific island but was, as Jim and Jodi were soon to discover, very much in character.

She was followed by a slightly built, balding man in a suit and silver wire-rimmed glasses. He looked to be in his early forties. The captain, with Annapolis written all over him, was the last one off. He checked the hawsers to make certain they were tied to his satisfaction then joined the group now approaching Jodi and Jim.

Lothar Bohm extended his hand to Jim. "We missed you at our meeting on Kwaj. And this must be Doctor Larsen," he said, turning to Jodi and shaking her hand. "Doctor Chambers told us about your mishap. I'm glad to see you came out unscathed.

"Let me introduce you to everyone."

Jodi and Jim were introduced first to Jeanne Raymond and then to Amos Whittier, the Surgeon General's representative. Whittier, the short, balding man, was an epidemiologist, an odd choice Jim thought, given the nature of their visit.

But Jim's attention was focused on the man to whom the captain had tossed the stern line. Although he had appeared younger at first, Jim could now tell he was about the same age as Bohm. And like Bohm, he wore a tee shirt and khaki shorts.

"This is Roy Stone," said Bohm. "Mister Stone is with the National Security Council."

"Pleasure," said Stone, his green eyes fixing Jim and Jodi in a way that made them both uncomfortable. A prominent scar on the right side of his face above the lip made him seem to have a continuous smirk.

"National Security Council?" Jim asked, surprised. "Sounds serious," he said, trying to maintain an air of nonchalance.

Stone laughed as if they were sharing a joke, but he said nothing.

After introducing the captain, a man named Nolan, and the young sailor, Everett, Lothar Bohm made an offer. "As you can see, we have a nice craft here with more than enough room to accomodate you both while we're in port."

"Thank you," said Jodi, "but I should stay on the island in case of any emergencies."

"That's a generous offer," said Jim, "but I've grown accustomed to Illetto living. I think I'll stay where I am. Thank you though."

"Well, in any event," Bohm said, his eyes flitting from one to the other, "after we tour the island, I hope you'll join us for lunch on the boat."

Jodi and Jim led as the group explored the island, Jeanne Raymond maintaining her impeccable appearance while Amos Whittier, sweating profusely and obviously bothered by the midday heat, mopped his brow with his handkerchief. Finally, he removed his suit jacket. Roy Stone said little but Jim knew nothing escaped this man's attention. He listened attentively to everything and when visiting Jodi's clinic and hut, scrutinized the furniture, equipment and structures as if committing them to memory. They ended up at Lekoj Kel's store. Kel was sleeping soundly in his chair in the open doorway, head slumped to one side and mouth open.

"This man has the right idea," said Whittier. "The heat is terrible."

"It takes some getting used to," said Jim, hoping it would be uncomfortable enough to drive the group away quickly. Bohm and Stone, however, showed no sign of being fazed. Neither man even broke a sweat.

"It reminds me of Vietnam," said Stone with a slight drawl. "I like it."

"I find it tolerable," said Jeanne Raymond. "We had hot summers in Nevada when I was growing up. Not as humid, of course, but hot just the same."

"I'm from Corpus Christi," said Stone amiably. "Nothing dry about our summers or winters. Just a matter of wet and wetter."

"The fisherman with the damaged boat. Where does he live?" asked Bohm.

"His house is the one near the dock," Jodi answered.

"And he's the one who showed you his find?"

"Yes."

"Why did he bring it to you?" Stone asked, a tone of friendly curiosity in his voice.

"Probably because I'm a physician. Maybe he thought I'd have an explanation."

"And did you?" asked Bohm.

Jodi looked him in the eyes, betraying no emotion. "No. That's why I went to see Doctor Chambers."

"I'd like to talk to the man," said Bohm.

"None of the people here speak English," said Jodi. "I know a few words of the Marshallese language, but probably not enough to help you."

A smile flickered around Bohm's thin lips. "You're being modest, Doctor Larsen. Doctor Chambers tells me you're quite fluent."

"She's just being kind," said Jodi, turning away to hide the sudden blush on her cheeks.

Is there anything that woman didn't tell him? Jim thought, swallowing his anger.

"It doesn't matter," said Bohm, "we have an interpreter arriving from Ailinginae later this afternoon."

"What kinds of medical problems do you encounter here?" asked Amos Whittier.

"Diabetes, high blood pressure, thyroid nodules—the same as on most of the islands. If we could convince the islanders to go back to the old way of life, especially their diet, there would be far fewer health problems. The thyroid nodules are a different story."

"What about the children?" asked Jeanne Raymond forcefully, trying to change the subject.

"Well, diarrhea can be a problem at times. We try to educate the parents about sanitation. Then there are accidents—near-drownings, falls from trees, man-of-war stings. Many kids need dental care because of sugar in their diets. Unfortunately, there's no one to provide it."

"Except for the heat, it certainly seems to be a tropical paradise," said Whittier, mopping his brow.

"Yes," said Jodi, "but a radioactive one."

There was a moment of awkward silence. They're so damned unwilling to confront the truth, Jim thought.

"Well," said Captain Nolan, who had not taken part in the conversation until now, "I don't know about the rest of you, but I'm getting hungry and I think we could all use something cold to drink. Everett is preparing lunch, so why don't we head back to the boat."

On the boat, they took seats at a table set up on the deck beneath an awning. Captain Nolan, seated at the head, nodded to Everett who disappeared into the galley and returned with a tray of sandwiches, a pitcher of lemonade and a large bowl of fruit.

"We have tuna or chicken sandwiches and there's also Coke or water if anyone wants," announced the captain.

"I'm not terribly fond of either of those dishes," Secretary Raymond interrupted. "Would it be possible to have a salad? And is there Perrier or white wine? A spritzer would be very refreshing."

"I'm sure we can accomodate you," replied Captain Nolan. He turned to Everett. "Would you see to that, please."

Seemingly lulled by the gentle rocking of the boat, the group ate in silence. Jim noticed that Bohm and Stone often stared out toward the surf breaking on the reef.

"You mentioned Vietnam," Jim said to Stone, as they were served coffee. "Were you there during the war?"

He nodded. "I was with the Special Forces for two years. Interesting experience."

"Were you in the highlands?"

"For the first year. Working with the Montagnards, winning hearts and minds." He pronounced the last words theatrically, then laughed humorlessly. "Not that it changed anything."

"So, Doctor Newell," interrupted Lothar Bohm, "while you were diving, you didn't see any dolphins?"

Jim just shook his head to avoid a direct answer.

"I've seen the photographs," said Doctor Whittier, "and I've looked at the X-Rays. What's your theory, Doctor Newell?"

"Well, all we have to go on are a dolphin-like head and an almost human upper extremity. It doesn't tell us much, so anything we say is conjecture."

"But conjecture can be interesting," said Bohm, "and given the history of this area, it may not be fanciful. If you don't mind hearing my theory, Doctor Newell, we know we have a creature that's either human with dolphin-like attributes or a dolphin with human attributes. We can surmise that we're dealing with a mammal, a mutant form of a mammal, but not one that suddenly appeared out of the sky—or water. Will you grant me that?" He looked directly at Jim.

"You have the floor, Doctor, and I'm listening."

"We all know these islands were exposed to heavy fallout from H-Bomb Bravo. Furthermore, we know genetic damage can occur from large doses of radiation."

"Our government didn't include Illetto among the islands it said were exposed," said Jim.

"We can put that aside," Bohm replied with a dismissive gesture.

"Our government also said its studies have shown no genetic damage. I've seen all the DOE reports," Jim persisted, turning to Secretary Raymond. "We know there has been an increase in thyroid problems but nowhere does it say anything about genetic damage. I've attended lectures by Doctor Chambers and she herself says the same thing—no genetic damage."

My God, thought Jodi, her eyes wide with surprise, I can't believe he's saying this with a straight face.

Roy Stone, too, had been watching Jim Newell carefully. "Doctor Newell," he said in a voice implying that Jim had had his little joke at their expense, "we all know our government says things that aren't always gospel. And I'm not saying there aren't good reasons. Now, I'm not a scientist, but I know that you don't believe a word you've said."

"All right," said Jim, "let's go back to conjecture. Even if there was genetic damage from radiation, how did that produce this creature? It's your scenario, Doctor Bohm, so I'd like to hear your explanation."

Jim now received the unmistakenly hostile stare he had been expecting. "My explanation? You already know that, Doctor Newell, since it happens to be your explanation."

"What are you talking about?"

"I have copies of your writings on inherited genetic damage. You and I both know that's what's involved here. There is no other explanation. When you were diving off Illetto, I believe you looked for dolphin schools which is exactly what I intend to do. Mister Stone and Secretary Raymond have provided me with classified data from the years immediately following Bravo. The Marshallese back then spoke of jellyfish babies. That information has never been corroborated but if it is true that there were abnormal births, then there is the possibility that some of them survived."

"In the ocean?" said Jim, hoping Bohm had no knowledge of the fetuses tossed into the sea.

"Why not? If there were births with the head of a dolphin, why couldn't they survive as marine mammals?"

Jim glanced over at Jodi and could sense her distress at how close Bohm was to the truth. She would have to speak to Mero again and to Mister Monna to caution against their mentioning the abnormal births on Illetto.

"That seems farfetched," Jim replied, finally.

"It's the only thing that makes sense. There had to be gradual evolution to make them more compatible with their aquatic environment. Why else the development of webbing? With the passage of enough time, these creatures would, I'm sure, become more like dolphins and less like humans."

"And how would you explain the underwater survival of helpless newborns?" Jim instantly regretted asking that question. Bohm was close enough to the truth without encouragement.

"I have to give that more thought. Perhaps dolphins played a role." Sitting back in his chair, he smiled crookedly at Jim. "You know, Doctor Newell, I can't help feeling you know more than you're letting on. I don't know why you would keep information from us, but . . . "

126

Bohm turned to Jodi. "Perhaps you, Doctor Larsen, could provide us with some insights."

"I don't really have anything to add."

"You were out with Doctor Newell on his dives?"

"On the boat, yes. But I don't scuba."

"I see. May I ask what you were looking for when your boat ran into trouble?"

"I was just out for a pleasure cruise. You've seen Illetto. There isn't much to do here with free time. There were few patients that day, so I took advantage of it."

"You know," said Jim, trying to be calm, "it's beginning to sound like we're being investigated. I don't understand. Since when does the discovery of a mutant creature warrant government department chiefs? And national security people? Could someone explain?"

"Doctor, I'll answer that for you," said Jeanne Raymond. "None of us would be here if we didn't think this was of vital importance. As I'm sure you're aware, we have a compact with the Marshallese government. That compact will be coming up for renewal soon. Our missile tracking bases in the Marshalls are the most important links in the defence of our country. We've had our difficulties with the Marshallese in the past. I'm not saying their anger wasn't warranted after the Bravo accident but we've gone out of our way to make amends. We've provided them with health care, footed the bill for medical evacuations to Hawaii, given them money and jobs. Still, there are troublemakers among them, people who would look for any excuse not to renew the compact, or who would bleed the United States for as much money as they could get.

"If word got out that there were monstrosities in the ocean, monsters created by fallout from American nuclear testing, you can imagine the uproar. There are many anti-nuclear groups, in America, Australia, Europe, all watching and waiting for their chance to put an end to our programs. The Japanese, in particular, have been a thorn in our sides.

"I want to be fair," she continued, "and I can understand how the Japanese feel after their World War II experiences. But they've come in here and tried to convince the Marshallese government that we're holding back information, that the health status of the islanders is more precarious than we've let on, all this while they're fishing out the

Marshallese waters and taking away a source of livelihood. The problem is they find officials willing to listen. All it does is drive the ante up. When the contract is renegotiated, there will be demands for more and more money.

"If the Japanese were ever to find out about the creature hit by that fisherman, it would be disastrous. That must be prevented at all costs."

Jim Newell, as he listened to this stylishly dressed Energy Secretary, felt she would certainly be right at home addressing a Senate Subcommittee meeting. There was a politician's zeal in her explanations. The phrase at all costs sounded particularly ominous.

Jim looked at everyone around the table. "It seems to me the arrival of a team of important American officials would be enough to provoke their interest, if they were to find out about it. We just have parts of one mutant creature. Does it warrant all this?"

"But how do we know there aren't more?" asked Roy Stone. "There could be dozens."

"Don't you think we would have known that before now?"

"We don't intend to make this a lifetime project, Doctor Newell," said Bohm, measuring his words. "But we do plan some intense searching. Then, if we find them, we'll be able to deal with the problem. Is there any reason you'd prefer not to help us?"

Jim knew his refusal was out of the question. "Of course I'll help. As long as you understand this is not an open-ended commitment. I have other obligations. And if you were to locate more of these creatures, what then? How would you deal with the problem, as you put it?"

Jodi watched intently, hanging on every word.

"We're putting the cart before the horse," said Bohm. "Let's find them first. That will be the hard part, won't it?" He put the question directly to Jim, who stared at him without answering.

"Why don't you bring your diving gear aboard, Doctor Newell. As soon as our interpreter shows up, we can talk to the fisherman and get out on the water."

By now Amos Whittier had dozed off in his chair, head on his chest and snoring lightly. Bohm stared at him, barely able to disguise his scorn.

"A little too hot for Doctor Whittier," said Jeanne Raymond, noticing Bohm's displeasure.

Jodi pushed her chair back, excusing herself. "I need to open the clinic," she said. "It's been a pleasure meeting all of you."

They all stood up, Jeanne Raymond thanking her for coming out.

"I'll get my diving gear," said Jim. "When do you expect your interpreter?"

"Within the hour," replied Bohm.

"In that case," Jim said, glancing at his watch, "I'll be back by four."

He followed Jodi down the ramp, then accompanied her to the clinic, neither one speaking until they were out of sight of the boat.

"There's something about Bohm that makes my skin crawl," Jodi said. "Am I imagining it?"

"If you are that makes two of us. It's like dealing with a snake. When you first see it you often can't tell if it's venomous. But if you pick it up and you've guessed wrong, that mistake can cost you."

"And Stone. What do you make of him?"

"Friendly on the surface. But he makes me as uncomfortable as Bohm. I don't like the whole situation, Jodi. But I don't know what we can do about it."

"There's always the chance they won't spot the dolphins."

"There's just as much chance they will. Bohm's not the type to give up easily. I think he'll persist until he does."

"And if they see the fish heads? Now that you've met them all, what do you think they would do?"

"You noticed Bohm wouldn't even discuss that. My guess is he and Stone plan to kill every fish head they find and send the remains to Washington."

"Oh, you can't mean it. Do you think Secretary Raymond and Doctor Whittier would go along with that?"

"Judging from Jeanne Raymond's speech about America's security needs, I think so. Whittier is an unknown quantity but he's not in their league. I can't imagine he'd have any real say. They'd all become part of a cover-up."

"Isn't there anything we can do?"

"The only thing I can think of is you'd better talk to Mero again and warn him that an interpreter is coming. He'll have to be careful about anything he says to you while that person is around. And make sure he and Mister Monna never mention that island where the women were. If you'll tell me how to say the words 'see Doctor Larsen now' in Marshallese, I'll send Mero up to you when I go back to the boat."

"That's easy. I hope he's at home. His boat wasn't there during lunch. He may be out testing it on the lagoon."

"Or he may be hiding. I'm sure he's no happier than we are to have these people around."

"This whole thing is senseless," Jodi said, exasperated. "I can understand their wanting to learn more about an unknown creature. And I can even understand concerns about political ramifications. But, let's face it, Jim, you and I, the only ones who really know more of these creatures exist, have only seen four. Stone thinks there might be dozens, but he's just guessing. And all these officials. I still don't know what they're doing here. Even if they spot a few of the creatures like we did, what good could it possibly do to eliminate them if that's what they have in mind? Do they plan on searching the entire Pacific Ocean to look for others? Some day another fisherman, off Pohnpei or Yap or Palau could run into one. Then what? They couldn't cover it up indefinitely."

"You're right, it doesn't make any sense. I don't understand how their minds work. Maybe they're only capable of thinking of what's best in the short term. Take care of the immediate problem and worry about the future later."

By now they had reached the clinic. No patients were waiting as they went inside.

"How ruthless do you think these people are?" Jodi asked suddenly.

"What do you mean?"

"I mean if they truly plan to cover this up, how do they know you and I won't tell what's happened? Or Mero, for that matter? The whole group, even Doctor Chambers, is connected with the government. I work for the Public Health Service, but that's different. There are only three of us who aren't part of their circle. I don't want to sound paranoid, but don't we represent a danger to them?"

"Others will know about this. They've sent the parts off to the Armed Forces Institute of Pathology."

"Another part of the government."

"I can't believe they'd . . . "

"But it's not outside the realm of possibility, Jim. Accidents—or what look like accidents—do happen. Stone was in the Special Forces in Vietnam. Even if he doesn't have blood on his hands already, I don't think he was picked for his national security job because he's a nice guy. And Bohm—Lothar Bohm—even his name makes me shudder."

Jim thought about Bohm's background. As much as he didn't want to believe it, perhaps there was truth in what Jodi was saying. To break his word to Mark Cantwell, however, and tell Jodi what he knew would only make her more anxious.

"I can't believe they would go to those lengths," he said, instead.

"You don't want to believe it—and neither do I. But we should keep it in mind."

She picked up a pad from her desk. "Here's what you say to Mero. It's short and I've written the words phonetically. Let's hear you say it."

Jim read it, making her laugh in spite of the situation. "Not bad," she said.

"I'd better head back," he said, pocketing the note. I'll get my gear on board but I don't think they'll have time to go looking for dolphins today. I'll be back as soon as I can."

"If you do go out, please be careful. Bohm and Stone will be diving, too, won't they?"

"I don't know about Stone, but Bohm will."

"Then you'll have more to worry about than just sharks."

"I'll keep that in mind," he said, heading for the door.

Jim took a different route and approached Mero's hut from the rear to avoid coming into view of the boat. One of the fisherman's sons, playing on the ground behind the house, spotted him and ran inside. Moments later, Mero appeared, nodded to Jim and shook hands. Jim removed the paper from his pocket and repeated the words slowly. Mero's face registered surprise. Whether it was because of his pronunciation or the message itself, Jim couldn't tell. But Mero quickly disappeared into the house, then reappeared and headed through the palms to the clinic.

Jim picked up his diving gear and retraced his own steps. Back on the regular path, he headed toward the boat. He could tell he was being watched by three men on the deck. Bohm and Stone he recognized.

"Our interpreter has arrived," Bohm said as Jim boarded. At that moment, Jim caught sight of a launch in the distance, growing smaller as it headed due east.

Jim shook hands with the short, dark man, a Marshallese introduced to him simply as John.

"We might as well go meet with the fisherman," said Bohm. "That's his house there, isn't it?" He pointed to Mero's hut, almost concealed in the dense greenery of the palms at the upper fringe of the beach.

"That's it," affirmed Jim.

As they headed for the ramp, Jim looked around. "Aren't Secretary Raymond and Doctor Whittier coming with us?"

"They're staying on board. The Secretary had some paperwork to complete and Whittier said he wanted to rest," Stone said. "The heat was too much for him."

Jim thought he detected a note of derision in the man's voice, but with that ever-present smirk it was difficult to tell.

As they reached the front door of the hut, Mero Attri was just coming down the path. "There's the fisherman," Jim said.

The Marshallese interpreter quickly stepped up and introduced everyone.

"Ask him to tell you about the day when his boat hit something in the water," said Bohm, wasting no time on pleasantries.

"He says he hit something and wasn't sure what it was, so he took it to Doctor Larsen."

"Were there dolphins in the area that day?"

"He says there may have been. He doesn't remember."

"Can he take us back to the spot?"

"He says he thinks so."

"He took Doctor Newell there, didn't he?"

"He said he took Doctor Newell to that area but doesn't know if it was the exact place."

"Well, tell him we'd like to go there. We still have almost two hours of daylight, so ask him if he'll come with us now."

"He says he will."

"Where is his fishing boat?" asked Roy Stone.

"He says he left it anchored in the lagoon. He wants to make sure it has no leaks before taking it out on the ocean."

"Why were he and Doctor Larsen out the day they hit the reef?" Bohm asked, his persistence after Jodi had already explained surprising Jim. Before he could protest, the interpreter relayed Mero's response.

"He says Doctor Larsen wanted to watch the sunset from the ocean."

Bohm, a hint of irritation in his voice, called to the captain to start the engines.

As soon as they were on board, Everett released the mooring lines and pulled up the ramp. Within moments, they were backing away from the dock.

Mero and the interpreter flanked the captain who, following the fisherman's instructions, steered the boat in a northeasterly direction. They were heading at least ninety degrees away from Mero's encounter with the fish head.

Jeanne Raymond and Amos Whittier soon appeared on deck, surprised to find the boat moving away from the island. Bohm and Stone ignored them, each scanning the surface of the ocean through binoculars.

Whittier approached Jim and cleared his throat. "Isn't it a little late in the day to begin our search?"

"The interpreter and the fisherman are both on board. I guess Bohm was anxious to get started," Jim replied, trying to sound detached.

Off to the northeast, miles in the distance, Jim watched as a rain shower developed from low-lying clouds. Above them, the sky was blue except for thin wispy clouds. The water's surface was unruffled by the light easterly winds. Bohm and Stone stayed near the bow, one on each side of the vessel, their attention riveted in front of them.

Mero Attri, standing next to the captain, turned for a moment and, catching Jim's eye, nodded imperceptibly. Good man, thought Jim, knowing how frustrating it must be for the Marshallese to be at sea without fishing lines in the water.

They were about five miles off shore when Bohm abandoned his post at the rail and walked up behind the captain. The boat slowly changed direction, heading more northwest. Jeanne Raymond and

Amos Whittier were now in deck chairs, a lively conversation occurring between them. For those two, Jim thought, this is nothing but a pleasure cruise.

Off their port bow, the sky had an orange glow as the sun dipped below the water's surface. Jim wondered how long they would stay out. At that moment they veered to the west and Jim realized Bohm had asked the captain to follow a wide arc before heading back.

Bohm and Stone were not the only ones scanning the ocean surface. Jim was more alert now as they approached the waters where he had seen the dolphins on his trips with Mero. When the bow finally turned to the southeast, Jim breathed a sigh of relief. He was looking forward to an evening with Jodi.

The dock was just coming into view when Bohm walked up.

"Quiet out there," he said.

"Well, it's a big ocean. At least we were able to enjoy the sunset."

"Will you join us for dinner?"

"No, thanks. I'll probably turn in early."

"We'll be heading out in the morning at eight. I've made arrangements for the fisherman to come along. Perhaps tomorrow we'll have a chance to do some diving."

"Tell Doctor Larsen she's welcome to join us," he called, as Jim headed down the ramp.

"Good night," Jim said, looking over his shoulder. Out of the corner of his eye, he spotted Roy Stone, standing in the ship's bow facing Mero Attri, the interpreter at his side. Jim paused, trying to overhear, but a sharp glance from Stone kept him moving. He wondered if they suspected anything. Even so, he thought, Mero wasn't one to be intimidated.

The only thing he and Mero had no control over was the dolphins. Tomorrow would be another nervewracking day at sea.

THIRTEEN

"Doctor, doctor."

Jodi's eyes flashed open. The first grey light of dawn was just coming through the windows.

"Doctor."

Jodi jumped up. "Coming," she replied, running her fingers through her hair.

At the door stood Mero Attri and Mister Monna.

Surprised, she asked them in. As they knelt on the floor mats, she heard Jim outside, softly calling her name.

"Mero and Mister Monna have just arrived," she said, opening the door to Jim and giving him a slight shoulder shrug which indicated that she did not know the purpose of their visit.

The two Marshallese shook his hand and they sat down.

Mister Monna spoke first and Jodi translated. "He says Mero is very worried. One of the men on the boat told him he would get in trouble and lose his fishing boat if he did not lead them to the dolphins. The man said they were on an important mission for the American government and he did not think Mero was being truthful with him."

"Damn him!" said Jim. "That was Stone."

"Mero is really frightened, Jim. They can't take his boat, can they?"

"Of course not. They're bluffing, just trying to frighten him. I was afraid Bohm might suspect something. Maybe he saw me talking to Mero before I sent him to see you."

Jodi conveyed Jim's reassurances but from their faces, they were not convinced.

"He says he doesn't want any harm to come to the dolphins but he doesn't want to lose his boat."

"I promise no one will take his boat. Tell him, too, that I won't be angry with him if we do spot the dolphins. I just didn't want him to head right out for the scene of the accident."

Jodi spoke rapidly with the two men for several minutes. She looked from one to the other before asking if they had any questions for Jim. They looked at one another and shook their heads, now more at ease. Again shaking hands with Jim and Jodi, they left.

"I told them you gave your word that Mero wouldn't get in any trouble. I told him, too, that he shouldn't be concerned if dolphins were spotted, that you would do everything possible to protect them."

"Well," said Jim, still angry about Stone's threats, "at least Mero knows nothing about what we saw down under, so he can't really tell them anything. Yesterday was a bust for them. I hope our luck holds today." He looked at his watch. "Almost seven. Let's have some coffee and I'll head over to the boat."

"I know how stressful this is for you," said Jodi, placing a hand on his arm. "You haven't had a chance to speak to the Energy Secretary or that other doctor, have you?"

"Those two won't be any help. You'd think they were on a pleasure cruise to Santa Catalina. I think they'll just defer to Bohm and Stone although Raymond lets them both know she outranks them."

As they sat around the fire drinking coffee, the sky slowly lightened. Plovers swooped low over the ocean and landed on the beach in front of them, skittering on stilt legs in graceful, darting movements.

Jim, staring into the distance, shook his head. "Even the weather is against us," he complained. "Too perfect. What we need are low clouds and heavy showers to cut visibility. Can't control the weather and can't control the movements of the dolphins. We'll just have to keep our fingers crossed."

"Remember what I said about the diving," Jodi cautioned.

"Don't worry. It's just too bad every paradise seems to attract its serpents. I'll see you tonight."

"With good news, I hope."

"That means with no news," said Jim, stroking her cheek and forcing a smile.

Jim could hear engines as he approached the dock. He was the last to board as Everett pulled the ramp up behind him.

"Good morning, doctor," said Everett cheerily. "Looks like we've got a beautiful day."

"Good morning, Everett. Yeah, it's a beautiful day all right." Jim tried not to frown.

Jeanne Raymond and Amos Whittier, seated on the deck, greeted him formally and then resumed their conversation about approaching congressional elections. Can they be oblivious to what's going on here? Newell wondered.

Bohm and Roy Stone, standing with the captain at the wheel, lifted their hands in greeting but otherwise ignored him. Mero Attri and the interpreter were standing at the bow. They turned and acknowledged Jim with a nod. Captain Nolan reversed the boat away from the dock then steered forward and swung around to the west. The boat rose and fell on the swell coming through the gap in the reef. Once through, he headed due north. Jim positioned himself at the rail within hearing distance.

The sun soon appeared off their starboard side, blinding in its intensity. Jim, shielding his eyes, turned in that direction. Everett came up to him with a cup of coffee. "Freshly made, sir."

Jim thanked the young sailor and focused on the water.

"It's beautiful this time of morning, isn't it?" Surprised, Jim turned to find Secretary Raymond at his side with Amos Whittier behind her.

"It is. Are you getting more accustomed to the heat?" he asked the doctor.

"Oh, yes," replied Whittier. "It's good to escape winter for a while."

"Doctor Bohm was rather upset last night," said Raymond.

"Oh? Why?" asked Jim, trying to sound casual.

"He thought the Marshallese fisherman had either forgotten where he had his encounter or was deliberately leading him away from the spot."

"Why would he do that?"

"I really don't know. That's what Doctor Whittier and I were discussing this morning. I can't see how it's possible to pinpoint anything on the water precisely and I certainly can't think of any reason for the man to send us in the wrong direction."

"What else did Doctor Bohm say?"

"He thinks dolphins will lead us to more of the creatures. If there are more of them," said Whittier, sounding skeptical.

"You don't believe there are?"

"I don't know for sure, but it seems to me if there were more of them, they would have turned up by now."

"Doctor Bohm is certain there are more," said Jeanne Raymond. "I think we'll have to trust his judgement." She turned away, heading toward Bohm and Stone.

Whittier, hands clasped behind his back, shifted his weight from one leg to the other as he balanced against the boat's jouncing.

"I wish we had some fishing gear," he said. "I'll bet these waters are loaded. Last year I went fishing in Chesapeake Bay and it was really disappointing. But here . . . " His voice trailed off.

Mero Attri would be happy to know there's a kindred soul on the boat, thought Jim. "I'm afraid all we're going to see today is a lot of water," he replied, hoping he was not mistaken.

"What's that island?" Roy Stone was asking the interpreter. He jerked his binoculars to his face with one hand and pointed with the other.

Jim quickly turned. In the distance, barely visible, was the island of evil.

"It's a small, uninhabited island," said the interpreter, relaying Mero Attri's reply. "It has no name."

As they continued their northerly course, a few seagulls were hovering above their wake. The sun was now high above them and Jim guessed they were at least fifteen miles out.

"Let's head northeast," directed Bohm. "We can follow that course for an hour or so and then begin a sweep to the west."

Another hour passed and Everett then called them to lunch. Only Bohm and the captain remained at the wheel. Roy Stone accompanied Secretary Raymond to the table, holding a chair for her.

"Everett," she said, "I'll have a white wine with ice. Seltzer on the side."

"Yes, ma'am. Let me just get Doctor Bohm and the captain their sandwiches."

She glanced over at the two standing rigidly at the wheel. Bohm lowered his binoculars as Everett approached. Bohm took the helm while the captain ate, keeping the boat on its northeasterly course.

After serving those at the table, Everett offered sandwiches to Mero and the interpreter, who were still in the bow.

Mild breezes did little to relieve the intensifying heat of midday. Not even coffee after lunch seemed to dispel the somnolence that overtook the gathering at the table.

"I'm going to have a nap," Whittier said, finally, standing.

"And I still have a report to work on," said Jeanne Raymond, following him below.

Without a word, Roy Stone got up and joined Bohm and the captain. Jim eased his chair around so he could watch them.

During the next few hours, Jim, lulled by the throb of the engine, caught himself drifting off but forced himself to stay awake. He finally got up and walked the length of the boat, keeping his gaze focused on the ocean surface or the men at the wheel. It was past three when Jean Raymond and Amos Whittier reappeared. Judging from the sun, Jim reckoned that they were headed due west. No islands were in sight. The water was calm and the seagulls had disappeared.

He must be getting frustrated by now, thought Jim, watching Bohm raise his binoculars every few minutes. It's about time for him to call it a day.

As if reading Jim's thoughts, Bohm leaned toward the captain, instructing him to change course. Realizing they were headed back, Jim relaxed.

Everett appeared with a tray of glasses which he set on the table. Secretary Raymond and Whittier immediately took seats and Jim joined them. Everett had returned to the galley for an ice bucket and lemonade. Reappearing, he asked Secretary Raymond, "May I bring you some white wine and seltzer?"

She answered without taking her eyes off the sea. "I'll have lemonade. Two cubes of ice and two twists of lemon. Is there vodka to mix with it?"

"Certainly, ma'am."

"Say, that sounds perfect," said Whittier. "Make that two."

At that moment, Roy Stone walked up.

"Oh, Mister Stone," said the Secretary, "I seem to have forgotten my sunglasses. I believe I left them on the dresser. Would you be so kind. It's the first cabin on the left."

Stone, his face darkening, glanced at Jim. He was obviously a man who did not like taking orders, especially from a woman. Amused, Jim couldn't suppress a barely perceptible smile.

Raymond and Whittier were into their second vodka as the sun settled slowly into the ocean off the starboard side. We must be getting close to Illetto, Jim thought anxiously, but there was no sign of land.

Suddenly, Bohm's voice boomed above the throb of the motors. "There!" he shouted.

They all sprang to their feet and looked where he was pointing. In the distance, more than a mile away, Jim detected movement on the ocean's surface. He knew from Bohm's excitement that it must be a school of dolphins. Bohm held his binoculars to his eyes as the captain quickly changed their course to southwest.

Jim checked his watch: almost 5:30. Time was the only thing he could rely on. It would be almost six by the time they reached the dolphins, too late to attempt a dive.

"Faster!" Bohm fairly screamed to the captain.

They could soon see the dolphins silhouetted against the mauve dusk as they leaped and arched from the water. But they moved steadily away from the boat bearing down on them, their silhouettes changing to slivers of black slashing the water as they fled.

The sun was now below the horizon. Bohm slowly lowered his binoculars and glared into the distance. Jim moved closer, waiting for his next move.

"Mark this spot, Captain. We'll resume our search here in the morning."

Jim clutched the rail tightly, his knuckles whitening. Mero Attri, standing behind the captain, turned toward him. Their glances met and Jim could see relief flitting in the black discs of his eyes.

It was dark when they reached Illetto. Captain Nolan slowly eased the boat against the dock with a soft thud. Lothar Bohm's voice rang out . "0700 tomorrow. That's seven AM, Doctor Newell," he called to Jim, who was already down the ramp. Those words were the only ones Bohm had addressed to Jim all day. The interpreter repeated the message for Mero Attri, who quickly followed Jim down the ramp.

"Goodnight, Doctor Newell," called Everett as he secured the boat's hawsers.

"Goodnight, Everett. See you tomorrow."

Jim shook hands with Mero, then headed toward Jodi's hut. The ground fairly rolled beneath him as he struggled to regain his land legs. Jodi had the fire going in the cooking pit.

She leaped up expectantly. "What happened?" she asked.

"Saved by the bell," Jim said with a smile.

FOURTEEN

"**How** do you pass your evenings, Doctor Newell?" asked Jeanne Raymond, coffee cup in hand as the boat pulled away from the dock the next morning. "A day at sea has me so restless I'm on pins and needles by eight o'clock."

"I like to get a swim in," Jim replied, trying to mask his nervousness. "But early bedtime is the norm for everyone on the island."

"Maybe we'll have good hunting today," interjected Amos Whittier, "now that we've had our first sighting."

Jim frowned. "Maybe," he said. "I don't think dolphins limit themselves to particular areas." Inwardly, he knew this was wishful thinking. The school that protected the fish heads definitely seemed to have a preferred area. Yesterday's sighting confirmed that.

For the next few hours Jim thought his luck might hold. In spite of their crisscrossing the northwestern region of the grid pattern worked out by Bohm, there was no sign of the dolphins. Meanwhile, like yesterday, Bohm and Stone huddled with the captain, barely acknowledging Jim's presence. Mero Attri sat glumly next to the interpreter on a bulkhead near the helm. Jim hoped that Bohm and Secretary Raymond were paying him for his time, time Mero could have put to better use. Jim paced the deck, staring out at the ocean.

Tradewinds, blowing from the northeast, had picked up, lifting whitecaps on the water. On the distant horizon rainclouds gathered but visibility was still unlimited. Bohm, Jim noted, seldom lowered the binoculars.

Roy Stone, standing to the right of Captain Nolan, suddenly grabbed Nolan's shoulder and pointed off the port bow. Lothar Bohm swung his binoculars in that direction. Quickly crossing to the port rail, Jim squinted to see what had caught their attention. But, except for a sooty tern swooping low over the water in the distance he could see only whitecaps.

The captain, on orders from Bohm, steered a course toward where Stone had pointed. They're grasping at straws, Jim thought. But then he saw it: an obvious disturbance on the surface. Ten minutes later, dolphins were plainly visible.

Jim's hands tightened on the rail. No descending twilight would save him today. The rain was many miles away and the boat was closing rapidly on the dolphins. But when they were about three hundred yards away the dolphins began leaping in unison, moving away to maintain their distance from the boat.

"I've never seen dolphins do that," Bohm said, turning to Jim. "Doctor Newell, what do you make of their behavior."

"It is strange. They seem to sense danger." He couldn't tell Bohm that this had happened before.

Mero Attri was now standing at the railing, his sour expression unchanged. He ignored the interpreter's questions.

Captain Nolan cut back the throttle, slowing the boat almost to a stop, throttling up just enough to avoid drifting. As they cut slowly through the water, winds rocked the craft.

"I'd better get some Dramamine," Jeanne Raymond said, disappearing below deck. Amos Whittier, his complexion almost green, followed.

The boat's slow speed seemed to calm the dolphins. No longer retreating, they circled, cavorting freely as the boat moved to within two hundred yards.

"Maintain slow speed," said Bohm, the binoculars now at his side. "I don't want to frighten them."

Jim anxiously watched as they approached. When they were barely two hundred feet from the swirling school, Captain Nolan, at a signal from Bohm, cut the engines. The splashes of the dolphins resounded in the sudden silence as some came nearer.

Bohm and Stone joined Jim at the rail. "We'd better get into our gear," said Bohm, looking at each of them as he uttered the words Jim had hoped never to hear.

Everett darted below to tell Raymond and Whittier about the dolphins. They all returned moments later.

As Jim opened his bag of diving equipment, Bohm removed two sets of gear and three tanks from the deck storage compartment. Bohm hadn't mentioned that Roy Stone was a diver, but Jim was not surprised. It must have been one of the prerequisites for his being chosen for this mission.

"Let's swim slowly," said Bohm. "Try not to do anything to frighten them."

Jim and Roy Stone followed Bohm to the stern. The three men then adjusted their weight belts and pulled on their fins.

"You go first," Bohm said to Stone, "then Doctor Newell. I'll follow."

As soon as Stone was in the water, Bohm motioned to Everett and handed him a spear gun. "Pass it to me when I'm in," he said.

The spear gun was utmost in Jim's mind as he rolled into the water. Ordinarily, he would not have given it a thought, especially in the shark-infested Pacific. But he would have to watch out for more than just sharks on this dive.

Roy Stone swam ahead of them. Jim slowed until Bohm was parallel. The school of dolphins was directly in front of them now, a mass of diving, arching and leaping black shapes.

The three divers approached slowly until they were about fifty feet away, then hovered in place. The dolphins were aware of their presence but showed no alarm. A few swam closer to inspect them, then fled, executing a series of acrobatic rolls to rejoin their companions.

Jim spotted a fish head immediately. Partially obscured by the dolphins, it moved slowly toward the surface with graceful motions. Suddenly, Bohm pointed excitedly. Three more of the creatures were plainly visible as they too swam for the surface.

With horror, Jim watched as his two companions floated motionlessly. He could only guess at what was going through their minds.

In a flash, one of the creatures, a male, broke away from the circle of dolphins, heading directly toward Roy Stone. The former Green Beret backpaddled vigorously, the camera clipped to his buoyancy control device forgotten. The creature then changed course and swam toward Jim.

They touched hands and Jim noted how its coarse texture was strangely at odds with its graceful movements. The fish head then turned toward Bohm, who remained motionless as the creature approached. It thrust a webbed hand out to Bohm but he did not respond. It was as if touching that hand would confer upon it a semblance of humanity or reveal a compassion that Jim knew Bohm was not capable of. The creature hovered before them and Jim could see that it was confused, an inquisitive expression clouding its eyes.

Then there was a sudden movement from Bohm. At first, Jim thought Bohm had changed his mind and was extending his hand toward the creature. But then he saw the spear gun. Jim instantly headed toward Bohm. The fish head, startled, twisted away. Bohm aimed the cocked gun, but just as he pulled the trigger Jim's hand struck his arm. The spear hurtled harmlessly toward the surface.

The dolphins, alarmed by the burst of the gun, fled, the fish heads protected in their midst.

Gripping the unloaded spear gun, Bohm shook his arm in anger toward Jim, then swam after the dolphins. Jim, his heart pumping wildly, started for the surface. Roy Stone, stunned by the altercation between the two men, hesitated, uncertain whether to follow Bohm or surface.

Jim pushed up his mask and shouted to Captain Nolan and Everett. Everett raced to the stern and leaned over, grasping Jim's hand to help him aboard. Mero Attri was staring wide-eyed as Jim stripped off his gear but Jim's attention was on the Energy Secretary and Whittier.

"Are the others okay?" called Captain Nolan.

Jim nodded. "Can we use your cabin for a brief conference?"

"Of course. Everett, clear my desk and take in extra chairs."

Secretary Raymond and Amos Whittier followed Jim below deck.

"I thought I'd fill you in before Bohm and Stone come back on board," he said as soon as Everett had closed the door behind him. "We saw four of them with the dolphins."

"You actually saw them?" Amos Whittier asked incredulously.

"One came up to us and Bohm shot at it with his spear gun. I knocked him off balance and he missed. Bohm was furious. The dolphins swam away but he followed them."

"Why did he try to shoot it? Was it attacking?" asked Jeanne Raymond.

"Attacking?" Jim snorted. "It touched my hand in greeting and was trying to do the same with Bohm."

"Then I don't understand."

"That makes two of us. You'll have to ask Bohm."

"We saw the dolphins moving off," said Whittier. "We thought something must have frightened them." He shook his head. "I wonder what got into Bohm."

"So these creatures really exist," mused Raymond as they headed back up to the deck. "Do they pose any threat?"

"None," assured Jim.

"Do you think the dolphins are protecting them?" asked Whittier.

"Yes."

As they left the captain's cabin and moved to the rail, they spotted Roy Stone fifty feet off the stern. Bohm trailed him by another hundred feet. Jim was glad he was too far away to see his face clearly. He could imagine the rage burning in his eyes. Suddenly, Jim saw the surface of the water agitate behind Bohm. A skim of foam spread out in concentric circles. Dolphins, he thought with amazement, they're circling back! Then, what he thought was the playful arc of a dolphin's flipper sliced the water. Jim squinted, unable to believe they would be trusting enough to approach Bohm again.

But then the ocean became still. Maybe they've turned back, Jim thought. Everett leaned over the stern to pull Stone onto the deck. Jim kept his eyes on Bohm's measured kicks. Suddenly, a fin sliced the surface right behind Bohm. With incredible speed it gained on him. There was no playful curve, no arc of spray.

Cupping his hands around his mouth, Jim shouted, "Bohm, shark!" Not waiting to see if Bohm had heard him, he lunged for his flippers and yanked them on. "Everett!" he yelled, grab my spear gun, there on the bench." By the time Jim hit the water, Everett was leaning over the stern, spear gun in hand. Jim grabbed it and with a powerful kick dived, heading toward Bohm.

Everett hollered for Captain Nolan and Stone who had gone below to store the empty oxygen tank. "Shark!" he yelled.

At that same moment, Bohm's scream rent the air and he disappeared below the waves.

Secretary Raymond and Doctor Whittier leaped from their seats, only to be shouldered aside by the captain as he rushed past.

Jim surfaced for air, still ten feet from Bohm. The tiger shark was plainly visible now, at least fifteen feet long, its sickle-shaped tail unmistakable as it thrashed the surface. Bohm struggled to free himself from the shark's grip even as it tore his flesh, ripping chunks from his thigh. A cloud of blood obscured Bohm as Jim fired his speargun, aiming at the pale gray underside of the shark as it rolled in front of him, Bohm helpless in its jaws.

The spear jolted the shark. It swung in a tight circle and released Bohm. Jim pushed powerfully with his fins, both legs thrusting together. Switching his gun to his left hand he made a grab for Bohm's vest, caught him and pulled his head above the water. He locked his right arm under Bohm's chin and braced his body against his chest as he back-stroked to the boat where Stone and Everett knelt in the stern, ready to pull them aboard.

"Oh, Jesus, he's bleeding to death!" Everett yelled as he hauled Bohm onto the deck.

"We need a tourniquet," Jim shouted as he dragged himself aboard and tore the flippers from his feet.

Bohm, unconscious, his skin ashen, was stretched out on the deck. He jerked convulsively with his lungs' explosive efforts to expel the salty water. The inner part of his right thigh was torn away. Blood pumped from severed femoral vessels, obscuring the wound as it welled up. A pool of blood rapidly spread beneath his hips, staining the polished teak deck that Everett had swabbed so meticulously that morning.

Jean Raymond, horrified, backed away, no longer the commanding presidential appointee demanding due regard. But then she fainted with an inarticulate gurgling, hitting her head on the rail as she collapsed.

"Never mind her!" Jim yelled, as Everett started to offer assistance.

Just then Captain Nolan bounded up from his cabin, first aid kit in hand. Jim grabbed a rubber tourniquet and with difficulty, stretched it around Bohm's upper thigh, glistening with blood.

"Radio Bikini," Jim ordered the captain. "Tell them to get a chopper to Illetto. How fast can we get there?"

"We're about a half-hour out, I figure, if we go full speed. Do you think he'll make it?"

"Not if we stand here talking. Go!"

Secretary Raymond had now regained consciousness. She stumbled back to the table, where Amos Whittier sat in numbed shock.

As they approached the island, the Navy helicopter, a bulky Huey, circled above, preparing to land on the beach. Jim knelt on the deck next to the unconscious Bohm, still alive, but barely. The tourniquet had stopped the bleeding but he was in shock, his thready pulse barely palpable.

Captain Nolan quickly maneuvered the boat up to the dock and Everett leaped off to secure the lines. Stone and Everett then helped Jim lift Bohm, secured on a makeshift stretcher Everett had devised from two mop handles and a bedsheet, over the port rail to the chopper crew that waited on the dock, arms raised to receive Bohm's unconscious form.

"We'll have to get him to Kwaj," Jim yelled to the pilot beneath the roar of the chopper blades. "I'll go with you."

As Jim was about to close the chopper's door, Roy Stone ducked under the rotors and planted himself in the doorway. "You bastard!" he growled. "If you hadn't interfered, we would have had that thing on board and none of this would have happened."

"Go to hell!" said Jim, slamming the door in his face.

FIFTEEN

Puzzled, Jodi looked up in the direction of the sound, but her view was blocked by coconut palms. It was not unusual for planes from Bikini station to follow a flight path over Illetto but she had never heard a helicopter before.

She hurried toward the beach adjoining the pier, the only patch of land clear enough for a helicopter to land. Emerging into the small clearing next to Mero's house, Jodi covered her face with her hand, bending away from the stinging sand driven by the rotors.

She glimpsed the boat moored at the dock. Men in flight suits rushed towards the chopper, trundling a stretcher between them. Jodi's heart jumped. Shielding her eyes, she squinted to see who they were carrying but she was too far away. Other islanders had now gathered, they, too, turning their faces from the whirling sand.

The pilot leaped from the chopper's cockpit. Doubled over to avoid the rotors' spin, he assisted the crew as they lifted the body into the helicopter. Another man clambered in and slammed the door. Moments later, the chopper was in the air, its rotors roaring. Jodi and the villagers turned their backs to the wind-driven sand, then looked up to follow the helicopter as it headed in a southeasterly direction over the island.

Jodi raced down to the beach, her heart pounding, looking for Jim. She spotted Roy Stone, huddled with Jeanne Raymond and Amos Whittier on the dock. Behind them were Captain Nolan and Everett. It was then that she saw Mero hurrying toward her.

"Mero!" she yelled. "What happened? Is Doctor Newell all right?"

"A shark attacked one of the divers. Doctor Newell jumped into the water and saved him. He went with him on the helicopter. They're taking him to the hospital on Kwajalein."

Relief flooded over her. Jodi wiped sand from her eyes with the back of her hand. Captain Nolan and Everett were now boarding the vessel. She watched horrified as Everett carried a mop and pail toward the stern. He leaned the mop against the rail, then splashed the bucket of water onto the deck. A foamy, blood-tinged froth sloshed over the deck and down the boat's side.

Jodi's legs tingled from shock as she approached the pier. Secretary Raymond stood erect, slightly apart from Doctor Whittier and Stone.

"God, it's so terrible," said Jodi. "Mero just told me."

"It was awful," said Jeanne Raymond. "Poor Doctor Bohm."

"I've never seen anything so courageous," said Amos Whittier, coming over to them. "Doctor Newell never thought of his own safety. He beat off the shark and brought Bohm back to the boat."

Roy Stone stared at Jodi. She couldn't decide if his look was hostile or if it was just her imagination.

"What happened before the shark attack?" she asked him.

"A great deal. I'm sure Newell will fill you in when he gets back. Please excuse me," he said, turning to Jeanne Raymond. "I'd better talk to Captain Nolan about our plans."

"What plans?" Doctor Whittier asked Secretary Raymond as Stone left.

"I don't know. We haven't had a chance to talk. We'd better get back on board. Will you join us, Doctor?"

"Perhaps later," said Jodi. "I have to be in the clinic this afternoon."

Jodi walked slowly as she left the beach, her thoughts racing. Stone's comment was puzzling. But it must refer to the creatures. Something else must have happened, something unexpected. Only Jim could tell her.

The hours in the clinic dragged slowly. Except for treating coral scrapes and removing sand particles from the eyes of some of the villagers who had been on the beach with her during the helicopter's visit, she had no interesting cases to distract her.

As dusk settled over the island Jodi went for a swim, hoping to dispel the fatigue that had followed the morning's excitement. Knowing Jim was safe should have been enough to renew her energy, but it wasn't. It was her relationship with Jim, or worrying what that relationship would lead to, that was sapping her strength. She had been doing just fine until Jim came to the island. Now that had changed. Any relationship, Jodi knew from experience, carried the risk of disappointment. Would it be different with Jim? As much as she dreaded it, she knew she was falling in love with him.

Returning home, Jodi prepared a light dinner of canned vegetables. Then she sat at her desk, an endocrinology text open in front of her. But it was impossible to concentrate. Her eyes drooped with fatigue and she read the same paragraph over and over again.

Jodi forced herself to stay awake, hoping Jim would radio her. But finally, she lay down on her cot and drifted off into a troubled sleep.

It was still dark when she woke. The luminous dials of her watch indicated it was only four. She listened to the sounds of the night, trying to pinpoint what awakened her. There was only the roll of the surf and the rustle of the palms in the ocean breeze. Jodi closed her eyes but knew sleep was hopeless. Suddenly wide awake, she threw on her shorts and a shirt and walked toward the beach. She would stay there, she decided, until the first streaks of dawn, then make coffee and watch the sun come up. She did her best thinking in the early morning hours.

She sat crosslegged on the beach, staring out at the black waters, the surf glinting an eerie white each time the moon appeared from behind the clouds. Suddenly, a beam of light flickered through the palms. She turned. Hidden from sight, she watched the light darting through the palms, edging closer to her hut. She knew it could not be a Marshallese. They did not use flashlights. Jodi hesitated, then flattened herself onto the sand watching the shadowy figure. He stopped outside the door, seeming to listen, then pushed the door open and stepped inside.

Jodi's heart pounded. No one on the island would dare enter her home like that. Frightened now, she lay still on the damp sand. Scarcely breathing, she waited. Minutes later the intruder emerged. He swung the flashlight beam in a wide arc toward the beach. At last the beam of light moved away through the trees.

She forced herself to sit up, chilled and shivering in the tropical night. It was probably someone from the boat trying to deliver a message, she thought, trying to reassure herself. But why wouldn't he have called out? She edged cautiously toward the hut. Once inside, she reached for her own flashlight beside her cot and scanned the room quickly with a narrow beam of light. Nothing was out of place.

Chiding herself now for having been frightened, she was determined to catch up with whomever it was. Holding her flashlight, she raced from the hut, following the path down which her visitor had gone. The moon provided enough light so she could see without the flashlight.

Approaching Mero's house, she again spotted the darting beam of light just ahead. Jodi paused.

The shadowy figure stopped outside Mero's hut as if listening for sounds within. Then, the figure knelt. In the stillness of the night, she heard the zipper on Jim's duffel bag opened. For almost a minute, the stranger squatted over Jim's equipment. If someone from the boat needed to borrow a piece of equipment, why not wait until daylight? she asked herself. She held her breath, barely able to control her fear. The throbbing in her head was excruciating and for the first time in her life she wondered if she was about to faint.

Just then the figure stood. He turned his head towards her, his face raised like an animal sniffing the night air. He was listening. Silently, he stepped in her direction, into the clearing. The ashen hair, scarred upper lip, and crudely chiseled cheekbones of Roy Stone were barely visible in the faint moonlight.

At that moment, the door of the hut opened and Mero stepped out. He glanced toward the water's edge and then went around to the side of the hut. Stone instantly crouched. Hidden in the shadows, he waited until Mero passed. Suddenly, a single sharp crack resounded, cutting the night's silence. Mero gasped and fell. Stone slid away from the hut, lithely treading toward the boat. He disappeared up the ramp, onto the darkened deck.

Paralyzed with fear, Jodi remained motionless. Her mouth tasted dry and metallic. She could barely swallow. Then Tima, Mero's wife emerged and spotted her husband crumpled on the ground. Kneeling by the body, she frantically shook him, sobbing and calling his name. Jodi quickly stepped out into the clearing and Tima let out a sharp, frightened cry. Recognizing Jodi, she fell into her arms. "Oh, Doctor Jodi, please come quickly. Something has happened to Mero."

"Tima, quiet! Don't make any noise. We're in danger. Someone broke into my house. I followed him here and saw him knock Mero to the ground. He boarded the boat but he may be watching."

"Who would hurt Mero?" she cried. "We were awakened by noises outside the house. Mero went out to see what it was and didn't come back."

Jodi looked down at the grotesque angle of Mero's head and knew immediately. His neck had been broken. She knelt next to him, pressing her fingers into his wrist for a pulse she knew was absent. Then, she rolled him onto his back. His head dangled like a useless appendage. Terrified, she wondered what to say, what to do.

Finally, she stood up and gripped Tima's arms. "He's dead, Tima. The man killed him."

Tima's hand flew to her mouth and her eyes rolled in her head. Jodi was afraid she would scream.

"Tima, listen, we've got to get help."

Jodi's first thought was to get help from the captain. But what if she ran into Stone instead?

Tima was shaking uncontrollably and Jodi took her in her arms. "Stay calm. We need to get help."

Tima pointed a trembling finger. "My cousin lives there. Very close."

"Come, we'll go together. Quickly."

Minutes later they returned with Tima's cousin and his wife. They stared with shock at Mero's body.

"We must take him inside," Tima choked through her tears. "I don't want the children to see him like this when they wake up."

"I don't think we should move him," said Jodi. "The Marshallese police wouldn't want us to. We can cover him."

Tima's cousin quickly went into the house and returned with a large piece of burlap sacking, the kind Mero had used to caulk the hole in his boat when they had hit the reef. He covered the body while Tima squatted next to it, rocking back and forth in the arms of her cousin's wife.

"I'm going to put a radio call through to Bikini," said Jodi. "They'll contact the Marshallese police in Ailinginae. Can you come with me please," she asked Tima's cousin. "I'm afraid to go to my house alone."

As the first streaks of light were appearing in the eastern sky they paused at the door and listened. The room was empty. Jodi rushed to the radio but there was no power. She yanked open the battery compartment. The batteries were gone. She had no spares.

"We'll have to place a call from the boat," she said, thinking to herself that if they made enough noise, they would wake everyone and be safe.

But even before they reached Mero's hut, Jodi could hear the throb of the ship's engines. Entering the clearing, they could see the gleaming white stern of the boat as its bow plowed through the reef opening into the open waters of the Pacific.

SIXTEEN

It was past midnight and Jim was at Lothar Bohm's bedside.

Clyde Johnson, the surgeon at Kwajalein Hospital who amputated Bohm's leg, had just left. Bohm had not yet regained consciousness.

Jim had been surprised when Bohm survived the helicopter trip to Kwaj. An ambulance had been waiting at the airport.

Doctor Johnson, awaiting their arrival in the hospital's emergency room, shook his head after a cursory examination.

"Looks bad," he said. "As soon as we get some blood into him we'll get him to the OR. Anesthesia's ready to go."

"I'd like to go in with you," Jim said.

"Glad to have you. I've got Doctor Simmons here to assist but we can always use another pair of hands."

The second unit of blood was in when Doctor Johnson decided they could wait no longer. "Let's get him down there," he said to the nurse and orderly. "I've got two more units available and we'll type and cross for four more."

"Any hope of saving the leg?" asked Jim.

"None. The femorals are shredded beyond repair and there's two much tissue damage. His only chance is a high amputation and even then it'll take a miracle to pull him through."

Clyde Johnson worked quickly and Jim was impressed with the man's skill. After receiving two more units of blood during the amputation, Bohm's blood pressure stabilized and his pulse was stronger.

After surgery, Doctor Johnson sat with Jim in the dressing room. "Well, he survived the amputation but with all that trauma and blood loss we've got to worry about his kidney function. We're not equipped here to take care of a case like this. If he's to have any chance at all we've got to get him to Hawaii."

"How soon can you transfer him?"

"We'll get more blood into him and if he's stable by tomorrow afternoon we'll air evac him to Tripler. I'll contact the surgeons there right now." He paused and stared at Jim. "That must have been one hell of a shark."

"Tiger shark. At least a fifteen-footer."

Johnson shook his head. "It's the worst shark bite I've ever seen and I've been here ten years."

Jim rubbed his eyes to erase the memory of the last twenty-four hours. It had been a long day. And he couldn't suppress the anger he felt at Stone. That hostile attack as the chopper was taking off frankly scared him. No one had ever treated him that way.

He vented his low opinion of Stone to Virginia Chambers when she arrived at the hospital. She had rushed over as soon as she heard. Jim explained what had happened during the dive.

"I want you to be up front with me," Jim said. "I don't know what you told Bohm about the fish heads but whatever you told him he must have passed on to Stone. Did Bohm know about those abnormal births?"

Chambers shook her head. "I never even told Bohm that you and Doctor Larsen had seen the creatures. I was going to but his attitude put me off. But now they know the creatures exist."

"Yeah, they've seen them. I just can't understand about Stone. Who the hell is he anyway? I know he's with the National Security Council but not much else. DOE already had Bohm here and Secretary Raymond. Why Stone?"

Chambers was silent.

"You know something."

She looked around nervously. And then, convinced they were alone, she said: "After our meeting, the one you missed, Jeanne Raymond and I spoke privately. I've known her for years, you know. Even before she became Secretary. She was concerned about Stone, too. He's with the Agency, you know."

"The Agency?"

She lowered her voice. "CIA. Jeanne Raymond did some checking. What she learned made her very uncomfortable. He's not just some bureaucrat. He's been an operative for years, one of these shadowy people that no one really knows about. Her contact told her Stone had done counter-intelligence work in Vietnam and later in Salvador." She hesitated. "There's a rumor he was involved in the killing of that archbishop—Romero? It's just a rumor. People like Stone always have rumors swirling around them."

"I don't get it. Why would they send some—some hit man—out here because of some mutation?"

"Jeanne Raymond couldn't understand it either. She knows how important these bases are. But even so . . . She tried to find out from the National Security Council why Stone was coming along, but didn't get any answers, just that it was a security issue."

"I don't like it, Virginia. I didn't get along with Bohm. He wasn't the most pleasant character. But with Stone, it's different. We've never said much to one another, but I've always been uncomfortable around him. And then that incident on the helicopter. He looked at me with such hatred."

"I'm really sorry about all this. When I asked you to come here, I never imagined. . . "

"I'm not blaming you for anything. Look, after Bohm gets evacuated, I'm going back to Illetto, at least for a few days. But until then I'll be at the lodge. If you hear any news, call me. I'd sure like to know what Stone is planning."

"You know I'll call."

Virginia Chambers was true to her word. The following afternoon Jim had just returned to his room from the airport where Bohm had been placed aboard a direct Army flight to Honolulu. A nurse from Kwaj Hospital had been assigned to care for him on the flight.

Jim picked up the phone. "Newell here."

"Virginia Chambers. I just spoke to Secretary Raymond. She was calling from the airport on Roi-Namur where she, Doctor Whittier, and Stone are catching the next flight to Kwaj. Stone wants me at a meeting at my office tonight at eight. I'll call you when it's over."

"I was thinking of trying to catch the last flight out to Roi today and then heading for Bikini, but I better find out what's going on first. I'll plan on being in my room from eight on. Thanks, Virginia."

That evening, Virginia Chambers sat opposite a grim-faced Roy Stone. Secretary Raymond and Amos Whittier were also seated at the table.

"We're sorry to have missed seeing Doctor Bohm," said the Secretary.

"It wouldn't have mattered," said Doctor Chambers. "I understand he was still unconscious. From what the surgeon says, it's a miracle he's still alive."

"You know Doctor Bohm and I saw the creatures during our dive?" asked Stone.

Chambers hesitated. "Yes, I do."

"Who told you?"

"Doctor Newell."

"Did he also tell you if it hadn't been for his interference none of this would have happened to Doctor Bohm?"

Amos Whittier cleared his throat, then removed his glasses and began cleaning them with his handkerchief.

"Do you have something to say?" Stone asked.

"I don't understand why Doctor Bohm tried to shoot the creature. It meant no harm."

"Why? Think, Doctor Whittier. We had the chance to take a specimen back with us. Our scientists could have studied it."

"But these creatures are almost human. Doctor Newell said they were friendly. It would have been murder to . . . "

"Murder?" sneered Stone. "These things aren't human! They're monstrosities!"

Amos Whittier flinched.

Secretary Raymond, also shaken by Stone's outburst, interrupted. "I feel it would be best to discuss this matter with authorities in Washington. We now know there are at least four of these creatures. We need guidance on how to proceed."

"We already know how to proceed."

"I don't understand," said Raymond.

"My superiors on the National Security Council are aware of what's going on. I spent a good part of the afternoon on the phone with them."

"And they've made a decision?"

"Yes."

All eyes were on Stone.

"You know what could happen if word gets out about these creatures. Every anti-nuke group in the world will descend upon us.

Every nuclear power plant will be in danger of being shut down. The outcry would make the anti-Vietnam war demonstrations look like a picnic. And the renewal of our compact with the Marshallese would be placed in jeopardy. That could cost us our major missile tracking bases in the Pacific and jeopardize national security. So what I have to say is never to get out of this room."

"I have a question," said Doctor Whittier. "If all this is top secret, what would you have done if Doctor Bohm had killed the creature? How would you have kept that from the Marshallese and the boat's crew?"

"Easy. Bohm and I would have bagged it and everyone would have thought it was a dolphin taken for research purposes. Any further questions?"

There was only an uncomfortable silence. Stone coldly scanned the room. "We're all agreed then?"

There was no reply.

"I'll take that as an affirmative," he said. "The creatures are going to be dispatched."

"Dispatched?" said Whittier, a puzzled look on his face.

"Eliminated, Doctor. I can't make it any clearer than that."

Amos Whittier sat rigid in his chair. Confrontation was something he had avoided during his entire life. But this proposal was simply wrong.

"I can't go along with this. It's immoral. I'm afraid I'll have to discuss it with the Surgeon General."

"That won't be possible. You were sent here as the Surgeon General's delegate. The only thing Doctor Mapes knows about this is that we were sent here to investigate a possible radiation-induced anomaly. He knows nothing about the existence of these monstrosities. But you do, and nothing discussed here can leave this room. If there's a leak of any information, it will be tantamount to treason."

Doctor Whittier looked around the table, hoping to receive some support from Secretary Raymond or Doctor Chambers.

"That's extreme," Jeanne Raymond snapped. "Perhaps if your superiors knew more of the facts . . . "

"This is a direct order from my superiors," Stone said icily.

Virginia Chambers stared at her hands, resting in her lap. Never, in all the years she had participated in the Marshall Islands study, had she experienced anything like this. She had viewed the problems of islanders exposed to nuclear fallout with scientific objectivity. But finding and arranging treatment for thyroid nodules and cancers was a far cry from participating in murder. Yes, from what she had seen and heard, maybe these creatures were horrible in appearance, monstrosities. But one of her patients on the island of Ebeye was also a monstrosity. The damage to that man's thyroid gland occured in his mother's womb and went undetected until some time after his birth. Now, whenever Dr. Chambers saw the man, crawling on his hands and knees, contorted, drooling, imbecilic, she was physically repulsed. So were the other physicians on the medical teams sent out by Haverbrook. But no one proposed the elimination, the murder, of this abnormal being. He was cared for and protected by the villagers. She knew she should speak up, but remained silent.

"Did Washington give you any idea how they propose to carry out this elimination?" Secretary Raymond asked indignantly.

For several moments, Roy Stone said nothing. He looked at all of them before he spoke. "A team of Navy SEALS will be sent to Kwajalein from Honolulu. Their base will be Bikini. I'm sure they'll be able to locate the dolphin school. How they carry out their assignment will be up to them."

"When will they arrive?" asked Doctor Chambers, finding her voice.

"They'll be here Wednesday and heading for Bikini the next day. I know you're anxious to get back to Boston, Doctor, and I see no reason for you to be here when they come. You can plan on leaving as soon as you wish."

He then looked at Secretary Raymond and Doctor Whittier. "I'll head back to Illetto and wait there. You can both return to Honolulu with Doctor Chambers and catch your flight to Washington. I'll keep you apprised of what's going on."

"I feel it's only fair to advise you, Mister Stone, that I cannot become a part of this," said Secretary Raymond. "It's outrageous. I plan to see the President personally as soon as I get to Washington."

Roy Stone stared at her and then grinned. "Secretary Raymond, see the President if you like. But maybe you didn't hear what I said. About my superiors on the Council? Who do you think made the decision? So by all means, see the President. I'm sure he'll appreciate having his orders questioned by his Energy Secretary."

Amos Whittier slumped in his chair. Any further argument was hopeless.

The light drizzle became a steady rain as Virginia Chambers pedalled back to her trailer. Her mouth was set grimly. She paid little heed to the rain. A few cyclists leaving the club rode quickly past her. By the time she arrived at her trailer, she felt like an old woman: old and weighted down.

She removed her wet clothes, hung them in the bathroom, and slipped on her robe before sitting down heavily on the sofa. She stared into space, listening to the steady hum of the air conditioner.

Everyone knew Virginia Chambers was a woman who lived for her work. No conversation, whether about politics or the arts or simple gossip, could be sustained for long without Doctor Chambers bringing it back to medicine. But people did not know that work was the dam holding an emotional flood that threatened to carry her away. That dam had been breached this evening by Roy Stone, by his dispassionate defence of murder under the guise of guarding the country's security. It reminded her of one of the shibboleths of America's jungle war in the sixties—we had to destroy the village to save it. And whenever Virginia Chambers thought of Vietnam, she thought not only of her own experiences there, but of Tom Lassen, the man who was to be her husband.

After Tom had died in 1964, she found that immersing herself in work kept her memories at bay. But tonight she saw Tom's face and heard his reassuring voice as clearly as if he were still standing with her in Logan Airport, awaiting his flight to San Antonio and the beginning of his basic training. He had just completed his internship and, with America's deepening involvement in southeast Asia and ever increasing need for physicians to treat the casualties there, had been drafted immediately.

"But look at the bright side, Ginny," he said, as she clung to him in the boarding area, " by the time I complete my two years in the Army, you'll be finishing your internship. The timing couldn't be better. We'll both begin our residencies at the same time and, if we're lucky, in the same hospital."

He had wanted to marry her before he left but she had convinced him to wait until he finished his military obligation. She had not known at the time that she was pregnant. Tom was still in San Antonio, halfway through his basic training, when she found out. She decided to say nothing. It would just be another burden for Tom to carry with him to Vietnam. She decided to wait until he had been overseas for several months before telling him. It would give him something to look forward to. When his year in Vietnam was up, they could be married. She knew eyebrows would be raised at the medical school as her pregnancy began to show, but Virginia Chambers was not one to care about what other people thought.

Tom's exhilirated response after receiving Virginia's letter about his impending fatherhood helped assuage the loneliness she felt. She was already six months into her pregnancy and Tom, in less than two months, would be halfway through his tour. His letters focused on their future together. There was little mention of the war. References to Vietnam mentioned the lushness of the countryside, the perseverance of the people and, above all, the beauty of the children. Virginia had loved to read his poignant descriptions of the street urchins in Saigon and in the hamlets of the countryside. It was as if the coming birth of his own child had awakened in him an awareness of all children.

And then, when she was in her eighth month, Tom's letters stopped. She waited nervously, hoping it was just the mails. As the weeks passed, her anxiety was replaced with dread. Finally, she called Tom's parents in Salisbury, Connecticut. She had met them only twice, and always formally. She did not even know if Tom had told them about their engagement or her pregnancy.

Tom's mother answered.

"This is Virginia Chambers," she had said. "I'm a friend of Tom's. I don't know if you remember me."

"Yes, I believe we met."

"I haven't received any mail from Tom in quite a while. I was wondering if you had heard from him."

The silence at the other end of the line told her everything.

"We received a telegram a week ago that Tom was killed in a mortar attack on his aid station. They'll be returning his body to us."

The woman's voice was controlled, like a tightly wound spring. Then her own voice cracked as she began to weep.

"Are you all right?" the woman asked.

Virginia put the phone down without saying another word. She wandered through her apartment in a daze, her hands unconsciously rubbing her distended belly. Mechanically, she looked at her watch. She was now in her last year of medical school and, ironically, doing an obstetrical clerkship. She was due on the ward in fifteen minutes.

She did not remember walking to the hospital or getting on the elevator. The nurse on duty at the obstetrical desk greeted her. "You've got a busy night ahead of you. Two multips in labor and one primip almost six centimeters."

"I'll check them," she said, her voice flat.

"Are you okay?" the nurse asked.

She nodded and walked to the first labor room. After examining the two patients, she came out into the hallway. At that moment, a cramp doubled her over. She gripped her stomach with one hand and supported herself against the wall with the other. False labor, she thought, trying to reassure herself, but the pain continued. Still bent over, she felt a trickle of blood running down the inside of her legs.

At that moment, the nurse at the desk looked up.

"Oh, my God!" She yelled for the other nurse and quickly helped Virginia to a bed. "Call Doctor Winters. He's in the doctors' lounge. Tell him it's an emergency."

Doctor Winters, a first year resident, examined her and dashed to the telephone on the nurses' desk. There was a frenzy of activity but Virginia could only focus on the pain in her abdomen. As if from a distance she heard the words abruptio placentae, type and crossmatch, immediate C-section.

Someone held her hand as she was wheeled into the operating room. For a moment, she thought she was still talking to Tom's mother. She cried aloud as the pain became unbearable but at the same time welcomed it. It kept her from remembering.

"Just breathe this, it's oxygen," the anesthesiologist said. And then a blast of color rose behind her eyes and she heard a roaring in her ears. She saw Tom's face disintegrating into fragments.

The light blinded her as she opened her eyes.

"Where am I?"

"You're in the recovery room. In a few minutes you'll be going back to the ward."

An intravenous tube was in one arm. Virginia stretched her free hand over her abdomen. It was no longer a bulging mound.

"Is the baby all right?"

"Doctor Rothman, the attending, will talk to you when you're in your room. You'll be more awake then."

She closed her eyes and when she opened them, she was in a dimly lit room. The bed next to hers was empty. The door opened and Doctor Rothman, a physician she had accompanied several times on his morning rounds, came into the room.

"How are you feeling, Virginia?" He pulled up a chair.

"I've been better. What happened?"

"You had an abruptio, a complete separation of the placenta. We're replacing some of the blood you lost. We'll have to keep an eye on your clotting factors for a while."

"And the baby?"

He shook his head. "I'm sorry, Virginia, the baby was dead."

"What was it?" Her voice seemed to be coming from far away.

"It was a girl." He cleared his throat. "The baby had spina bifida, Virginia. She would never have walked. Perhaps this was all for the best."

"All for the best," she had murmured.

SEVENTEEN

It was getting late and Jim had given up on hearing from Virginia Chambers. He was just getting into bed when his phone rang.

"Doctor Newell, it's me. We have to meet."

"We have a bad connection," he said, barely recognizing her voice.

"I can hear you," she said.

"What time tomorrow morning?"

"It can't wait. I'm leaving for the States tomorrow."

"You want to meet me now?"

"Yes, at the Japanese cemetery. I'll meet you outside."

Before he could ask why she wanted to meet at such a remote location, she hung up.

Puzzled and apprehensive, Jim was soon on his way. It was almost eleven o'clock and the streets were deserted. The small cemetery was in a relatively isolated area not far from the landing strip. He parked his bike next to the white picket fence surrounding the lawn. A simple pagoda-like arch had Japanese Cemetery written in English and Japanese. A marble memorial stood in the center of the grassy area, a mass grave for the Japanese soldiers killed in the World War II battle for Kwajalein.

Minutes later, Virginia Chambers arrived. Her face was haggard and her eyes puffy, prominent wrinkles radiating from the dark shadows under her lower lids. Even the stiff smile was absent. This was not the Virginia Chambers he knew.

"Let's get out of the light," she said. "I don't want anyone to see us."

He followed her into the shadows behind the memorial.

"Are you all right?" Jim asked. "You look tired."

She didn't answer.

"So you'll be going home tomorrow," Jim added, trying to put her at ease.

"Yes, home," she said, as if she had forgotten what home was. "Jim, I have to tell you about the meeting at the hospital."

He was surprised. This was the first time she had called him by his first name.

"There were four of us—Stone, Secretary Raymond, Doctor Whittier, and myself. Stone said he'd been in touch with Washington."

"Did he say what they intend to do?"

"A team of Navy SEALS will be arriving here in Kwaj, then leaving for Bikini."

"This is getting ridiculous. Now Stone wants the SEALS to confirm what he saw?"

Doctor Chambers looked down at the ground, then raised her eyes and stared directly into his. "Not confirmation. They want the SEALS to kill those creatures."

"I can't believe it. What kind of people are they? We can't let that happen."

"We were sworn to secrecy during that meeting."

"The Energy Secretary and Doctor Whittier went along with that insane plan?"

"They weren't happy about it, but they didn't have a choice. They'll be flying to Honolulu with me and then back to Washington."

"What do you mean they didn't have a choice?"

"When Jean Raymond said she was going directly to the President, Stone laughed at her. He said the order to kill the creatures came from his superiors on the National Security Council. He implied they came from the President himself."

Jim shook his head slowly, an agonized expression on his face. "We can't let this happen. There must be something we can do. Someone we can talk to."

"If word gets out, they'll know the leak came from someone in that room. Stone said that would be considered treason. I'm telling you because I trust you. And I wanted to warn you about Stone. He said he's going to Illetto to wait for the SEALS.

"I feel responsible for having dragged you into this. I don't want you to get into any trouble. Stone resents you. The man is ruthless. I know you have to go back to Illetto, but I don't think you should be there when he is."

"Did he say when he's going?"

"No. It could be any time."

"I'm heading back tomorrow. I tried to place a radio call to Jodi—Doctor Larsen—while you were at your meeting, but her radio was dead. I'm worried something is wrong."

"Probably just something mechanical. What will you do when you get there?"

"I don't know. This is Doctor Larsen's last week on the island. You probably know by now that I'm very fond of her. I was going to head back to the States when she left Illetto."

"I'm glad something good came out of this. Well, it's getting late and I have a lot of loose ends to finish up in the morning. I'll have you booked on the first available flight to Roi-Namur tomorrow and then arrange your Bikini flight. You'll hear from me by eight o'clock. And think about what I said, Jim. I don't think you should be there when Stone arrives."

"I appreciate your being honest with me."

"You'll call me at Haverbrook when you get back home?"

"I'll call."

She rode away, a hunched, lonely figure disappearing into the darkness. With her veneer of self-confidence gone, Jim had looked deeply into a wounded soul. She had stuck her neck out for him. But what would he do with this information? And what could he expect from Roy Stone?

Mounting his bicycle, Jim paused to stare at the Japanese monument. He wondered if his actions would be as futile as those of these nameless Japanese soldiers who died defending these lonely chunks of coral in the middle of the Pacific Ocean.

EIGHTEEN

"**Busy** day for me," yelled the young sailor over the roar of the launch's engine. "First time I've had to make this trip twice in the same day."

Jim threw him a surprised look. "You've already made a run today?"

"Yeah, with a guy who came in on the first flight from Roi."

That was the plane Jim had hoped to take, but Virginia Chambers said she couldn't get him on a flight until noon.

"Who was this guy?"

"Civilian. Said he's with some scientific team."

"What did he look like?" Jim asked, already knowing the answer.

"Ordinary looking guy, except for the scar on his lip."

Troubled, Jim pondered the sailor's revelation. He stared at the faint outline of Illetto, the palms along the shore just visible in the distance. The sun had already sunk below the western horizon and dusk spread like a stain across the sky. Roy Stone was already on the island.

"Strange thing," said the sailor.

"What's that?"

"He wanted to be let off on the southern tip of the island. I told him there was no place there for me to get him up to the beach but he said it didn't matter, he'd wade in. And that's what he did. Carrying a bag of diving gear."

If Jim had been concerned before, he was now frankly worried. Why was Stone trying to hide his arrival on the island? Why wasn't Jodi's radio working? Too much was happening that he didn't like.

"Can this thing go any faster?"

"I've got it wide open, Doc. We'll be there in a few minutes."

Jim sprang from the boat onto Mero's pier. "Thanks," he yelled to the sailor, who waved as he backed away from the dock. Mero's boat lay on the beach, its hull listing sideways in the sand. Jim glanced towards Mero's hut, expecting to see the children playing outside, but a strange quiet hung over the place. It almost looked abandoned, but his diving gear was where he had left it, against the side of the house.

Jim rushed along the path, dark now in the twilight dusk. Jodi's house was deserted. He called out, but there was no answer. The ashes in the fire pit were cold. He scanned the beach behind the house, but there was no sign of her.

Newell was sweating now, more from worry than from the heat. He headed for Kel's store. There, sitting in his usual chair, was the storeowner. He jumped up as Jim entered and shook his hand, chattering excitedly.

"Where is Doctor Jodi?" asked Jim.

"Come," Kel said, leading him to the hut out back.

He's misunderstood, thought Jim, until Kel knocked and Jodi opened the door.

"God, I'm happy to see you," she said, embracing him.

"What are you doing here? What's wrong? Your radio isn't working."

She said a few words to Kel and he returned to the store. Again she hugged Jim. "Come, sit down. I'll tell you everything."

They sat on a woven rush mat on the floor, a kerosene lamp flickering nearby, while Jodi related all that had happened. Jim couldn't believe what he was hearing.

"I've been too afraid to go back to my house since then," Jodi said, "so Kel is letting me stay here."

"But why would Stone kill Mero? It doesn't make sense," he stammered, a stunned expression on his face.

"Remember what we talked about? Only three people outside the government loop who know about the creatures? Now there are only two."

"Can that bastard be so insane?" Even as he asked the question, Jim knew the answer. "He's here, he's on the island, Jodi."

"Who?"

"Stone. The sailor who brought me over on the launch told me he dropped Stone off earlier today."

"Oh, my God! That man is a killer and we don't even have a radio. Stone took my batteries. I couldn't even call Bikini after Mero's murder to get the Marshallese police here from Ailinginae. What are we going to do?"

"I think we'd better stay right here for now. Chambers stuck her neck out to warn me last night that Stone was returning to Illetto. I just didn't think he'd get here this fast. She told me Navy SEALS are being sent to Illetto to kill the creatures. All top secret. Where are Mero's wife and children?"

"With relatives on the island. Tima took the children right after we buried Mero."

"I have an idea for tomorrow. Where is Tima staying?"

"With her cousin. It's very near her own house. What are you thinking?"

"We can take Mero's boat and get help on Bikini. I'm sure I can get us there."

"I wonder where Stone is now," said Jodi.

"I don't know. Does Kel know what's going on?"

"He knows Mero was murdered. The whole island is in a state of shock. Nothing like that has ever happened here."

That night, stretched out on the floor mats, they slept restlessly, listening for any sound that was out of the ordinary. Kel had given them knives, which gave Jim some sense of assurance. In the early hours of the morning, when Jodi's hand reached out and found his, they were able to sleep for a few hours.

A rooster's crowing awakened them at dawn. Their fingers were still locked together.

"It's not even six," said Jim. "Do you think it's too early to tell Tima our plans?"

"I'm sure she's awake. I'd feel better if we get an early start."

Jim opened the door slowly, scanning the nearby surroundings. It had rained during the night and water dripped from the bushes and palms. The only sound was Kel's snoring from the nearby hut. Jodi, carrying a small tote bag she had stocked with water, sun block, and a few items of clothing, followed him outside.

Tima was already outside her cousin's hut with her sons, the baby suckling contentedly at her breast. Her dark face normally framed a bright smile but now it was drawn, her mourning evident. They told her they were taking Mero's boat to get help.

Then, Jim and Jodi headed for Mero's hut. They passed the fresh mound of earth and sand where Mero was buried, a rudimentary wooden cross starkly marking the grave. Jim paused for a few moments and stared sadly down at the grave. They approached the house warily, looking all around them. Jim knelt to inspect his diving equipment, then looked up to find Jodi watching him, her face pale.

"What's the matter?"

"I saw Stone kneel there by your bag just like you're doing before he killed Mero. It reminded me."

Jim, frowning, held up his camera. The back was open. "The film's gone. Looks like Stone doesn't want any photos around. No evidence. No witnesses." He then examined his spear gun. "At least this seems fine."

They quickly placed their gear in the center of Mero's boat and pushed it through the fine, soft sand toward the water's edge. Jim, soon standing waist deep in water, held the boat steady while Jodi grabbed the edge of the craft and climbed in.

Suddenly, a figure emerged from the palm trees along the beach and loped toward them. Jim dropped the bow rope and crouched defensively in the water. Jody, alarmed by Jim's quick movement, swung around on her seat.

"Good morning," Roy Stone said, mock friendliness contrasting with the steely look on his face. "I've always enjoyed early morning boat rides." He carried a small sports bag, giving him the appearance of a man hurrying to the gym for a morning workout.

"Sorry," said Jim, immediately pushing the boat into deeper water. "You're not invited."

"You don't understand, Doctor. I'm in charge now." Stone's hand darted into his sports bag and with one smooth motion, he had pulled out a .357 Magnum, its stainless steel barrel glinting in the morning light. He cocked the hammer and pointed the muzzle at Jodi's head as he quickly waded to the boat and pulled himself in.

"Come aboard, Doctor. You two sit in the stern. Let's go."

"Where are we going?"

"I'll let you know when we get there. Start the engine and let's get moving."

Jim slowly lowered the outboard's propeller into the water and pulled the cord. It started, as it always had for Mero, on the first pull. He steered toward the break in the reef. The orange glow in the eastern sky signalled the beginning of what would have been a beautiful morning. Jodi sat rigidly, her eyes riveted on the weapon in Stone's hand. Jim, all his senses at peak, noticed his bag of diving equipment between her right leg and the hull.

"Why did you kill Mero?" he asked, hoping to distract their captor.

Stone's eyes focused on Jodi. "Did you tell him that? I thought you might have seen me." He smiled maliciously. "Well, I was watching, too. I spotted you and that native woman from the ship. It doesn't matter. Why did I kill him?" He turned to Jim. "Because he came snooping around while I was taking the film out of your camera. But he would have had to die sooner or later anyway. He was the only one on the island who knew about the monsters—except for you two, of course."

"So you're planning to kill us, too?"

"I don't kill—accidents happen. But you'll have the satisfaction of knowing you're dying to protect your country's security."

"You're forgeting about the others—Chambers, Raymond, Whittier. Are you going to kill them, too?"

"I don't have to. They won't break their oath of silence. And they're too afraid to ruin their careers over something like this."

"And how will you explain our disappearance?"

"I won't have to. I never saw you. This boat will be found capsized near the reef. You seem to have bad luck when you're around reefs, don't you, Doctor Larsen?"

Jodi, repelled by his smile, lowered her eyes.

"Yes, the widow will tell everyone that you went out together on the boat. I watched you this morning, just like last night, Doctor Newell. I know how you two spent the night—it was pleasant, I hope. Unfortunately, that's the last night you'll spend together."

Jim, more alert than he'd ever been in his life, glanced over his shoulder. Illetto had receded into the distance. To his right, the sun sat perched on the ocean's rim, its warmth flooding over them. He had to keep Stone talking. He'd flatter him, annoy him, do whatever it took to distract him.

"You're pretty clever."

"I leave nothing to chance, Doctor. I told you I'd been with Special Forces in Vietnam. During my second year, I did counter-insurgency work. To do that successfully, you have to anticipate your enemy's every move. Then, when the opportunity presents itself, you eliminate your adversary. It's very simple—and very effective."

"Yeah, I'll bet you did a lot of brave things, like throwing prisoners out of helicopters."

Stone gave a derisive laugh. "If I didn't know better, I'd say you're trying to get me angry."

"I saw how brave you were with that half-human creature. I wasn't impressed."

"I'm beginning to find you tedious, Doctor Newell. Slow down. This is as good a place as any."

Taking a chance, Jim lunged at the throttle. The boat lurched forward, responding immediately. Jim had always wondered about Mero's engine. Too much power for this size boat, he had thought. Now he put it to good use. Jim swung the boat sharply to port. Stone lost his balance just as he fired. The bullet shattered the rim of the hull next to Jim. "Jodi, the speargun," Jim yelled, quickly turning the boat in the opposite direction.

Jodi snatched the speargun from Jim's bag. Instinctively snuggling her index finger around the trigger, she pointed the gun at Stone. He raised his revolver and Jodi pulled the trigger.

Stone fell backward, the spear embedded in his neck just above the collarbone. His head hit the the bow with a thud as the revolver spun out of his hand into the water.

Jim cut back on the throttle as Jodi sat frozen, staring at Stone. His body slumped backwards, legs spread, the spear dangling almost limply from his neck.

"I've killed him. I've killed him,"Jodi cried, her eyes wide with horror.

Jim turned toward her calmly. "He was going to kill us. You saved our lives."

"What are we going to do?" She began to weep quietly.

Jim stared at Roy Stone's body, blood now staining his shirt. "Take over the engine," he said.

With one yank, Jim wrenched the spear from Stone's neck. He washed the spear carefully in the water, then replaced it in his bag. Still kneeling, he turned to Jodi.

"Do you remember what Stone said? He never saw us. Well, we never saw him either. What happened here was self-defence, but where's his weapon? Gone. It's better this way, Jodi. We never saw him. We'll just continue on to Bikini as we planned."

"You mean we just . . . "

"Yes."

"But what about the SEALS?"

"Jodi, Mero's dead. Stone's dead. Bohm, if he survives, will never swim again and you and I will be gone. It's over."

Without another word, Jim lifted Roy Stone's legs and heaved the body backwards, headfirst into the water. The boat lurched for a moment, then righted itself.

Jodi turned in disgust. "God, Jim, are you sure he was dead?"

"If he wasn't, he is now," Jim replied coldly. "What did you want me to do, Jodi? Call 911? That bastard was going to kill us."

Jodi shielded her eyes from the sun's glare and scanned the water. There was no trace of Roy Stone.

Jim took control of the boat and quietly watched Jodi, who sat motionless, cradling her head in her hands. He touched her shoulder lightly, hoping she would take some comfort from the contact. Ahead of them, he could just discern the shape of the buildings on Bikini atoll, less than an hour away, the sun glinting off the tin roofs like a beacon.

Jodi stared at the ocean behind them. "It's so still," she said.

"It's best to forget what happened, Jodi."

But at that moment, the silvery gray form of a bottle-nosed dolphin leaped from the water where Stone's body had disappeared. It was followed by another and then another.

"My God, Jim!" Jodi cried. "The dolphins are back. It's as if they know they're safe now."

Jim turned just as the dolphins disappeared beneath the surface. He then opened the throttle to full speed and placed an arm around Jodi.

Far behind them, Roy Stone thrashed helplessly beneath the surface, weak from loss of blood. He was conscious, aware that he was drowning. Sharks, drawn by the scent of blood, were approaching.

The dolphins were agitated, roiling the waters above him. They circled, swimming faster and faster, forming a protective ring around the dying man. The largest, a pewter-gray male with a cream-colored belly, dived beneath him. Acting as if from instinct, it forced its snout against Stone's body and pushed him toward the surface. The others followed the big male's lead, prodding and pushing. Stone's head soon broke the surface and he gasped for air. As he started to sink, the male swept beneath him, using its powerful body to force him up. Stone flailed helplessly, vomiting salt water and struggling to breathe. The big male glided slowly beneath the surface, its tail barely moving as Stone, lying prone on the dolphin's back, clung precariously. The dolphin raised his head mere inches above the water to spout, his every movement deliberate so as not to dislodge his cargo.

Three dolphins broke away from the protective circle around Stone and hurtled through the water as the first sharks appeared. But the big male, as if guided by an internal compass, swam slowly and steadily in a southeasterly direction, aware only of the frail passenger on his back whose life depended on him.

*****

The Kyuko, a Japanese fishing trawler, had had a good run. The crew emptied a net full of tuna onto the deck and crew members in rubber boots sloshed through the mass of fish, shovelling them toward the almost full hold.

Captain Tanaka set their course back to the processing ship, the Tsukiji, anchored forty miles to the west, where the cargo would be unloaded. He raised his binoculars and adjusted the focus, trying to make out a disturbance on the ocean's surface off his port bow.

"Look, look there! Are those dolphins?" he called to Namura, his first mate, who was leaning against the control panel smoking a cigarette.

He passed the binoculars to Namura and swung the wheel to take them toward the dolphins.

"It looks like a body!" Namura exclaimed, lowering the binoculars and rubbing his eyes. He raised the binoculars again. "It's surrounded by dolphins."

Tanaka stuck his hand out. "Give me the binoculars."

He peered through them again. "Yes, I can see it now. It's a man. Tell the men to lower the dinghy," he ordered.

Captain Tanaka cut the engine. Namura raced down the metal steps leading from the wheelhouse to the deck, calling to Kurame and Shimada, the first two men he saw. "There's a body in the water," he shouted, leading them to the rail. "Lower the dinghy and bring it in."

The two men yelled to their companions on the deck. They lowered the boat into the sea, the two crewmen already in position on their seats. Shimada and Kurame rowed toward Stone. The dinghy bobbed smoothly over the soft swells. Stone, barely conscious, had wrapped his arms around the dolphin's neck, one side of his face resting on the dolphin's sleek back.

Shimada dropped his oars in the locks and reached over the side of the dinghy. He grasped Stone's arm with one hand and grabbed a handful of wet teeshirt, hauling him into the boat. Kurame set his weight on the opposite side to balance the small craft.

The moment Stone's body was lifted from its back, the big dolphin disappeared beneath the surface. He then surfaced one last time, as if to reassure himself that the man was safe, then raced in leaping, gleaming parabolas toward his mates.

The trawler moved cautiously alongside the dinghy. Crewmembers lowered a sling of canvas straps over the side to cradle Stone's body and lifted him onto the Kyuko's deck.

"He's still breathing," Namura said, kneeling in a puddle of blood-tinged water that spread beneath Stone's body.

"Carry him to my cabin," shouted Tanaka, coming down from the wheelhouse. "Wrap him in blankets and stay with him. I'll radio the Tsukiji."

Namura was sitting on the captain's bunk next to Stone when Tanaka entered. In the cabin's dim light, Stone's face was pale from blood loss. His eyes were closed and frothy blood bubbled from his lips.

"How is he?" Tanaka asked.

"Alive. Not conscious."

"Does he have any identification?"

"Nothing in his pockets."

"Maybe the Americans in Kwajalein can help."

*****

At three o' clock that afternoon, Roy Stone, wrapped in Army-issue blankets, lay on a stretcher, an intravenous plasma drip in one arm.

"Can you hear me?" the medic asked over the din of the helicopter.

Stone, his eyes closed, did not respond.

"Are you American?"

"Stone nodded.

"What happened to you?"

"Accident. Spear gun."

"Where's your boat?"

Stone didn't answer.

"Okay, don't worry. We'll have you in the hospital on Kwaj in a flash. The Japanese fishermen told us the dolphins saved your life. That's a new one. You'll probably be air evacked to Hawaii, you lucky dog."

Ignoring the medic, Stone slowly opened his eyes and turned his head toward the light streaming through the helicopter window. But all he could see in the stark brightness and what he would remember for the rest of his life were the eyes staring at him from the watery depths as he clung to the body of his unlikely rescuer.